Intimate Measures

Stepping back, he eyed her hips consideringly. "I could lend you a pair of jeans. Let's take a closer measurement," Rune murmured, drawing her against him and then sliding his hands from his own hips to hers. "I think we could work something out here, don't you?"

His voice grew muffled as he buried his face in her throat, and with a desperate half laugh, Corey pushed against his chest. "Remember what happened the *last* time we started fooling around. Don't tempt fate, Rune."

"Don't tempt *me*, darling," he returned, sliding his hands up her back.

Dear Reader:

SILHOUETTE DESIRE is an exciting new line of contemporary romances from Silhouette Books. During the past year, many Silhouette readers have written in telling us what other types of stories they'd like to read from Silhouette, and we've kept these comments and suggestions in mind in developing SILHOUETTE DESIRE.

DESIREs feature all of the elements you like to see in a romance, plus a more sensual, provocative story. So if you want to experience all the excitement, passion and joy of falling in love, then SIL-HOUETTE DESIRE is for you.

Karen Solem
Editor-in-Chief
Silhouette Books

DIXIE BROWNING
Matchmaker's Moon

Silhouette Desire

Published by Silhouette Books New York

America's Publisher of Contemporary Romance

SILHOUETTE BOOKS
300 E. 42nd St., New York, N.Y. 10017

Copyright 1985 by Dixie Browning

Distributed by Pocket Books

ISBN: 0-373-05212-X

First Silhouette Books printing June, 1985

10 9 8 7 6 5 4 3 2 1

America's Publisher of Contemporary Romance

Printed in the U.S.A.

DIXIE BROWNING

is a native of North Carolina. When she isn't traveling to research her books, she divides time between her home in Winston-Salem and her cottage at Buxton on Hatteras Island.

1

Corey recognized the two cottages immediately. "Squatty and gray, just like me" had been her cousin Abbie's description.

At the moment, Corey was feeling pretty squatty and gray herself—emotionally squatty and gray, at any rate. At five-foot-seven-and-a-half, she could hardly qualify as really squatty. She'd always been lean, and since the day late last spring when her life had started coming apart at the seams, she'd grown even more slender. As for the gray, she'd yanked out another one just this morning. It was truly frightening the way a woman could slide downhill so gradually that she never even knew what was happening until one day she woke up and found herself out of the game. Obsolete. Redundant. Squatty and gray.

Forcing herself into a more cheerful frame of mind,

Corey whipped her small Chrysler into the double drive-way that served Abbie's two cottages. Maybe she'd take over the spare, she thought in a burst of tired whimsy. The two of them could spend their twilight years rocking on the screened porch and watching the gulls fight over tidbits left by the outgoing tide.

As she nosed her car up close to a tall privacy fence, she caught a glimpse of sparkling turquoise. The swimming pool. Installed by the original owner, it was both expensive to maintain and totally unnecessary, according to Abbie, but when Corey had received the call asking her to house-sit the cottage while Abbie went on a European tour with a group of retired fellow school teachers, it had been the mention of the pool that had tipped the scales.

Step number three in her make-over, Corey had decided on the spot, would be a deep, sexy all-over tan. For years she'd settled for the bits and pieces she'd managed to get on the run.

June heat slammed into her like a hard fist when she stepped from the air-conditioned car, and she sighed and surrendered the last of her makeup to the perspiration that quickly filmed her face. Every stop between Morristown and Emerald Isle had taken its toll; by now her once-neat traveling outfit was a wreck. She'd never really liked the snap-front cotton dress, but it was practical enough, and the price had certainly been right. Since Edwin's sporting goods store had started carrying the line, it had become her uniform on the rare occasions when jeans wouldn't do.

She reached into the backseat for the largest suitcase. "No more practical wash and wear," she muttered, swearing as the thick wad of hair she'd pinned so neatly on top of her head that morning at the motel began to slither down the back of her neck. "Unless it's this damned head of hair!"

Step four, she vowed silently, would be a haircut— something simple and cool, but terribly chic. Something that didn't reek of Morristown's one and only salon.

"Abbie, I'm here," she called out as she began lining up her luggage on the sandy concrete drive.

"Corey?" The familiar voice of her favorite cousin came from the screened porch, and then Abbie was hurrying down the wooden steps, plump arms outstretched in a welcoming gesture that brought stinging tears to Corey's gray eyes. Abbie's bedrock wisdom had been all that had held her together over this past year.

"Oh, Abbie," she wailed, and flung herself at the shorter woman, laughing, crying, hugging tightly, in spite of the heat and humidity that made flesh stick to flesh. "Why'd you have to move all the way from Missouri to the ends of the earth? I thought I was never going to get here!"

"Honey, come on inside and let me look at you; your bags can wait. You look tired, and you've lost too much weight. I haven't seen you in—my land, it's been almost three years! How's Winnie? Did you two get everything patched up before you left?"

"Golly, it's good to see you, Abbie. You're right, I'm bushed, and I'd just as soon not hear how I look. Honestly, your timing is incredible! I was climbing the walls back in Morristown."

"That bad, huh?"

Grimacing, Corey nodded. "You know, I can still remember the day you left home to move to Raleigh. I thought you were crossing the Atlantic and I'd never see you again, but you've always been there when I needed you." Her eyes blessed this dearest of all her relatives. In spite of the fact that they were separated by almost thirty years, they'd always been close. "Abbie," Corey cried suddenly. "What on earth happened to your head?"

The older woman touched her glowing orange hair tentatively. "What do you think—too obvious? When you told me over the phone you were going to do a complete make-over on yourself, it set me to thinking. I've been gray since I was forty, but there's no reason on God's green earth why I have to stay that way. I had it done yesterday. What's more, I've got this cream that's guaranteed to get rid of all my liver spots. And I finally broke down and bought myself a genuine silk dress. Looks pretty good on me, too. It's red with a purple sort of splatter all over it, and I found some purple shoes that don't hurt too much."

Corey's smile didn't waver. Who was she to say that orange hair and a red silk dress wouldn't work miracles? Her own dull, suburban taste hadn't earned her any notable rewards. "It must be a phase of the moon or something," she said. "I went on a spree, too. I've got two suitcases full of the most outrageously impractical clothes you've ever seen. I spent a whole weekend in St. Louis shopping for resort wear after you called."

Abbie's shrewd gaze dropped to the wrinkled cotton dress, and Corey protested quickly. "Strictly a leftover from the past. I knew this trip was going to be a bruiser, so I thought I'd give one final fling to my old PTA-and-town-meeting dress before I cut it up for dust rags. Not that I intend to spend much time dusting," she added. "Believe me, in the few months before it actually happens, I'm going to give new meaning to the word *hedonist*. Remember the tank tops and boxer shorts I used to wear? Wait till you see my new bathing suits."

"Finally broke down and got yourself a bikini?"

Shaking her head, Corey laughed. "Thank goodness your pool's got a fence around it. I'm still not quite sure you don't have to have a permit to wear the things I got. They're cut *up* as far as possible and *down* as far as possible."

"Fences won't keep the sun out," Abbie remarked dryly. "Just be sure you don't blister your 'possible.'" She led the way inside a shady screened porch to where a pitcher of iced tea and two glasses waited. "If I know you, yours hasn't seen the light of day since your mother used to bathe you in a dishpan in the backyard. This sun can ruin you if you don't take it in easy stages." She poured two glasses of iced tea and settled into a rump-sprung wicker rocker. "Sit, honey. You look washed out. How'd you leave things with Winnie?"

Shoulders slumping dejectedly, Corey said, "I don't particularly want to talk about it."

Absently, Abbie scratched a mosquito bite on her left ankle with her right toe. "Suit yourself. She's your daughter, and you know what they say about the apple not falling far from the tree. Your Daddy had his heart set on your going to the university. When you and Edwin up and ran off and got married right in the middle of college . . . I hate to say it, honey, but—"

"Then, don't. Please." Corey groaned and leaned forward, resting her cheek against the frosted glass. "The things Dr. Spock never told us about raising a child. At least I was married when I got pregnant. And I finally got my degree."

11

"An associate degree," Abbie reminded her with the superiority of someone with a Masters in education. "And you were married exactly nine months and two days when Winnie was born. You could have ruined your whole life, Corey. I taught high school kids for thirty-two years, and God knows, I've seen some messes you wouldn't believe."

"Tell me about it," Corey agreed dolefully. "If I hadn't been so sold on the idea that nice girls *didn't*, I wouldn't have been in such an all-fired hurry to get married."

"But then you wouldn't have had Winnie, and don't tell me you don't love that child, Corey Murchison Peters, because I've known you since the day you came squalling and red-faced into this world."

"Abbie, since last spring . . ." Corey thumbed a forefinger and began to enumerate. "My husband dumped me to marry a twenty-four-year-old bubblehead." She thumbed the next finger. "My daughter announced that she had no intention of going to college, never mind that I'd already sewn in a thousand name tapes, and that incidentally, she's three months pregnant and if it's all the same to me, she'll take her college money for a wedding present."

The familiar blind panic threatened to engulf her once more, and ruthlessly, Corey shoved it away. "Abbie, in less than three years I'll be forty. My husband didn't want me, my daughter doesn't need me, and damn it, I'm going to be a *grandmother!*" She stood up and began to prowl, fingering a shell ashtray here, a cork-based hurricane lamp there. "I don't know what happened—I blinked my eyes for a second and my whole life whizzed past."

Abbie noisily filtered the last of her tea through the ice

cubes and then placed the glass on the floor. "You're looking for sympathy from sixty-six-and-still-single? Forget it, girl. At least you had a whack at it."

"A whack! One day I'm cheerfully washing socks for a husband and consoling a daughter whose biggest concern is whether or not the braces will be off in time for the homecoming dance. The next thing I know, I'm picking myself up off the floor and wondering what hit me. Damn it, Abbie, I don't *deserve* this! I practically ran every charitable organization in town. I was class mother three times, I was a Brownie leader, I organized the Maple Street Mothers Patrol, and—"

"And while you were busy being Saint Corey, your husband was chasing everything in skirts and your little girl grew up. So where's your gumption? All the Murchison women have taken their licks and come up fighting, from the time Great-great-grandma Rebecca defied the whole town of Cape Girardeau to take in three Cherokee children whose parents had died on the Trail of Tears, and then lost 'em all to smallpox."

Corey had been raised on the story of her headstrong ancestress. "Oh, Abbie, I know it's happening all the time—divorce, teenage pregnancy. But when it's happening to you, it's different. I just need more time to get used to the changes in my life, that's all."

"The only reason you and Winnie can't get along together right now is that you're too much alike. You were just like her when you were her age, only back then, we hadn't been through the sexual revolution. Nowadays it's no crime to get pregnant before you get married. Stupid, maybe, but no crime."

The wicker rocker clicked on an uneven board, and Corey sat down again. "Abbie, why is it that a few words from you always seems to put my life back on track, no matter how botched up it is? Remember when Ed got fired and we lost the house and had to move into that awful apartment? You told me then that no door ever closes without another one's opening."

The most subtle of smiles came and went on the weathered face. "Have I ever lied to you? There's an open door in front of you, honey, and all you have to do is walk through it."

"The only door I see is marked grandmother and mother-in-law, and quite frankly, it doesn't look all that inviting. I guess I'm just selfish."

"Pshaw! You're better-looking now than you ever were, and what's more, you've got the freedom and the experience to enjoy it. Open the door!"

Locking her hands together, Corey stared at her knuckles. "And if there's a tiger behind it?"

"Tame him."

"That's easy for you to say," Corey scoffed. "Look at you now—four beachfront lots, two cottages with a swimming pool, and you're taking off tomorrow with a group of old friends on a European tour."

"Huh! Museums, historic sites, and cheap hotels. Dinner conversation will be a comparative analysis of laxatives and bridgework. Sounds exciting, doesn't it? And for that I get my hair done and buy a genuine silk dress?" She grunted expressively. "I don't want to think about it, so tell me more about this make-over of yours. Frankly, so far it doesn't show."

Pouring herself another glass of tea, Corey leaned back and began reciting the list that had begun as self-imposed mental therapy. "Item number one, get rid of the suburban housewife clothes. If I put a bag over my head, you

14

couldn't tell me from half the women in Morristown. Item number two, makeup. Until I went on my shopping binge, I owned two lipsticks, both in the same shade of pale nothing, and one pressed powder compact. I'd even run out of cologne and hadn't bothered to buy more."

She laughed, thinking of the hours she'd spent learning to apply the stuff she'd spent a small fortune on. "Let me tell you, I've got a paint box Michelangelo would have envied. Now, if only I can figure some way to keep it from melting as fast as I trowel it on. The tan should help; that's next on the list, by the way. With a tan, you don't need much more than a strategic dab of color."

"Right back where you started, then, aren't you?"

Corey shook her head slowly, a secret smile lighting her gray eyes like sun breaking through storm clouds. "Depends on the color—and the tan. I'm talking shimmering gold eye shadow, passion-bruised lips, and all-over oiled perfection, the kind of tan that lolls around swimming pools and sips tall, cool exotic-looking drinks from the hands of tall, cool exotic-looking men in white linen suits and Panama hats."

"Sounds like a James Bond movie," Abbie scoffed good-naturedly. "Just watch out you don't end up flat on your back with third-degree burns."

"If I end up flat on my back, it'll either be on a beach towel or on satin sheets."

"Hussy!" Abbie laughed and crunched an ice cube.

"I'm trying, I'm trying, but when you're as out of practice as I am, it's not easy."

"That's it? Paint, glad rags, satin sheets, and a third-degree burn?"

"I'm going to learn to drink something besides white wine. I'm going to read *Cosmo* instead of *Good House-*

keeping; I'm going to learn to eat snails; I'm going to cut my hair short and have an affair, and—"

"You're going to *what?*" Abbie's bare feet slapped the floor as her rocker lunged forward.

"Cut my hair?" Corey repeated, all innocence. "Abbie, I started wearing it this way—well, not exactly this way," she said with a grimace, shoving a pin back into the precariously balanced knot. "When I was first married, trying to look older. It's about time I—"

"Don't be smart, Missy; I've handled 'em bigger and tougher than you'll ever be. What's this business about an affair?"

"You're the one who told me to open that door and go for it. Don't worry, I'll be discreet."

"Discreet, my aching—! Corey, child, you haven't already done anything stupid, have you?"

"If you call refusing alimony stupid. If you call selling the house and settling most of the money on Winnie stupid."

"I'd call it wishful thinking, if you're still hoping she'll use it to get her degree, but that's not what I'm talking about and you know it."

"I only want her to have options, Abbie. She's too young, and I don't want her to feel trapped. The money will be there for her when and if she needs it. Or for the baby."

"All right, then, back to this affair you mentioned. I hope you haven't already—"

"Look, Abbie, I know you're trying to protect me, and I appreciate it, but believe me, if I'm ever going to find out how the other half lives, it's got to be now. I'm going to be a *grandmother* in six months, don't you understand? Don't you realize what that *means?*"

16

"It doesn't mean you're going to be embalmed, for pity's sake! Don't be so eager to rush into something temporary. Have a little patience, child; there might be something worth waiting for right around the corner."

"Abbie, I'm not rushing into anything, and I'm *certainly* not looking for another husband, if that's what you're hinting at. I've had a lot of time to think things through, and whatever I do, I'll do it deliberately, with my eyes wide open. Believe it or not, I stayed perfectly calm throughout this whole mess," she finished proudly.

At the other woman's skeptical look, Corey qualified the statement. "All right, so I blew off steam in a few letters."

"And cried a few gallons of tears over the phone," Abbie reminded her dryly.

"But when Ed moved out, I went right on with the plans for the children's home fund-raiser even though I knew damned well everybody in town was whispering about us. And then, when all this other business came out, I put on a lovely wedding for Winnie and Mike, complete with a reception. What's more, I made Edwin give them Winnie's whole college fund for a down payment on a house in River Hill. And dear God, I smiled until I thought my teeth were going to dry up and fall out."

"How'd Edwin behave? He didn't have the gall to bring that tart to the wedding, did he?"

"He knew I'd have yanked her bleached hair out," Corey declared grimly. "No, I probably wouldn't have wasted the energy. Lord knows, anything we'd had between us was over years ago. We were both so caught up in our own affairs, though, that I never even noticed."

"Well, *I* noticed. Half the time I called you, you'd be

there alone with Winnie, and he'd be off on some trumped-up excuse or another!"

"It's only good business when you sell sporting goods to go to all the games and tournaments and conventions. Besides, it was all a tax write-off. I probably should have gone with him, but I didn't feel like it when I was pregnant, and after the baby came . . ."

"If you'd gone, maybe he wouldn't have started fooling around."

"I never had a very high tolerance for all-night parties and high-stakes gambling, but Ed loves a crowd. He was Morristown's big football hero in high school, remember? Unfortunately, it was the high spot of his life, and he's been trying to recapture it ever since. Complete with cheerleaders." There was no bitterness in her tone. She'd long since gone through all the stages—the shocked disbelief, the outrage, the self-pity, the self-doubt, the guilt. Finally, she'd been able to offer genuine forgiveness.

Only Edwin hadn't given a damn for her forgiveness; all he'd wanted was his freedom to marry a woman who was twenty years younger than he.

"Will they live in Morristown?"

"Four blocks from our house. *Four blocks,* can you believe it? Honestly, Ab, that man has the sensitivity of a rusty nail! The house sold last week, thank goodness, so the final step in my make-over will be deciding where I'm going to relocate and what I'm going to do. Maybe I could rent your other cottage," she suggested half-seriously.

"Well now, we might work something out when I come back from this tour. The place is already leased for the summer, though."

"You mean I've got neighbors?" Corey tried to keep the dismay from showing. She'd hoped for more privacy. But then, she didn't have to socialize if she didn't want to. "I'd sort of counted on oiling up and getting down to basics behind your privacy fence, but I suppose your tenants have pool privileges?"

"Tenant, singular. You'll have plenty of privacy for your metamorphosis, if that's what you're worried about. Mr. McLaughlin won't be bothering you, but maybe I'd better warn you about my cat and his bird."

"Bird?" The vision of an elderly man living alone with his canary came to mind, and Corey began to relax again. "You told me about this antisocial tomcat of yours, so I can see where there might be a slight conflict of interests."

A hairpin struck the floor, and Corey caught the slithering bundle of hair in one hand and held its warm weight off her neck. "We'll get along just fine, Abbie; don't worry about a thing. If your Mr. McLaughlin will keep his canary under control, I'll see what I can do to restrain your cat. Where is he, by the way?"

"Parrot. He's a writer, you know. Keeps funny hours, but I reckon that's his prerogative as long as he pays the rent on time. Just don't forget that he lets the noisy, squawking thing out on the screened porch during the afternoon while he's sleeping. Jack has to be kept inside then, or he'll have the bird knocking his silly brains out."

Corey digested that bit of news. Her neighbor evidently took afternoon naps, which meant she'd be free to do her sunning then. "Sounds like a workable arrangement to me, but maybe you'd better leave me a schedule of what I do when—and to whom."

"I generally take a walk along the beach when the

bird's on the porch. What with the gulls and the crows and that damned mockingbird that eats my mulberries before I can get to 'em, it's bedlam for a few hours."

"Good. I'd planned to do a lot of beach walking, too. How's the mulberry crop?"

"Bumper, but you'll have to get up early to beat the birds."

An enormous yellow cat with a broad battered head wandered out and sniffed suspiciously at Corey's ankles before wrapping himself around Abbie's leg. "Don't worry about McLaughlin. You just go right on about your business as if he weren't even there."

The cat detached himself from his mistress and deigned to allow Corey to pet his arching back. As she did so, Corey glanced up to catch a look that could almost be described as gleeful on her cousin's weathered face. "Don't look so amazed. I told you I worked at the animal shelter two days a week back home, remember? Jack and I will get along just fine."

Abbie stood and brushed the cat hairs from her hands. "Glad to see you've still got a spark of gumption. Still like a challenge, don't you?"

She led the way into the house, and Corey stood to follow her, leaning over to give the cat one last stroke. "Why, you ungrateful stinker, you!" she cried, snatching back her hand, then examining the slight indentations.

"What's the matter, Jack take a chunk out of you?" Abbie switched on a ceiling fan and opened the refrigerator door to browse.

"Just a warning nip." Turning a grim smile on the cat, who was already occupying the chair she'd vacated, Corey said, "You wait, old fellow. One of us is going to back down, and it won't be me, I assure you. I've done all the backing I intend to do."

There were dozens of last-minute questions to be asked as they waited for Abbie's boarding call, and Corey knew there'd be dozens more once her cousin was out of reach.

"Look, don't worry about anything, Corey. You've got my itinerary—you know where to write. I'll send you a postcard if I decide to stay longer than six weeks."

"Longer!" Corey wailed. "What do you mean, longer?"

"I told you, stop worrying; I'll probably be back with the rest of the gang, but if I see something worth a second look, I might stay on a few more days. Was that my section they just called?" She stood and gathered her carryons. "Now remember, I don't consider a hurricane an emergency unless the eye passes directly over my house. I've left a list of numbers—the plumber, the electrician, and my doctor are in the back of the phone book under plumber, electrician, and doctor."

"I'll miss you, Abbie. Have fun and don't look back."

The two women embraced. "Good advice for both of us. Let's take it, shall we?"

Laughing, Corey called after her. "Where's the nearest good hairstylist? I can't wait to get on with my make-over!"

"Morehead City. Number's in the back of the book— ask for Milly. See you in a couple of months, honey. Be good."

A couple of months? Corey shook her head. Offhand, she couldn't think of a better way to spend a couple of months—or even the whole summer—than soaking up sun beside a swimming pool, catching up on years of reading, and taking long solitary walks on the beach. Sooner or later she was going to have to come to grips with her future. She couldn't just coast the rest of her life; she was a doer. Besides which, her resources were limited. Before her savings ran out completely, she was going to have to find some way to start earning a living for herself.

After seeing Abbie off, Corey checked the list of errands. Lately, her whole life seemed to have been made up of lists, as if a neat little list could lend meaning to the frightening hollowness of her existence.

At the bank, she arranged a transfer of funds and a temporary checking account. She needed groceries, but first she needed lunch. After passing two familiar hamburger franchises, she found what she wanted, a fastfood place that specialized in something she could never have found in Morristown.

Throwing caution to the winds, she ordered her first fried oyster sandwich and enjoyed every bite of it. Next time, she promised herself, she'd tackle a soft-shell crab sandwich, working her way up to the special of the house, a sharkburger.

Next came the supermarket, and she took her time getting acquainted with the layout, the specials, the prices, and the atmosphere. It was almost two before she pulled into the driveway again, and she heard the ruckus as soon as she opened the door. Surely no bird could make a sound like that.

"Come down from there, you carnivorous bastard!"

"Are you talking to me?" Corey asked, peering at the

pair of hairy, muscular legs suspended from the branches of the mulberry tree.

There was a grunt, followed by several ominous creaks and a series of highly inventive oaths. From the cottage next door, the harsh screams continued to rip the somnolent stillness of the otherwise peaceful afternoon.

"Look, if you want some mulberries, all you have to do is ask. There's a ladder around here someplace," Corey said in her most reasonable tone. In the yellow linen sheath dress, she was wilting rapidly. No telling what was happening to her groceries.

The legs descended abruptly, followed by a pair of white boxer shorts—the under variety, not the swimming variety. They were followed by a broad and naked chest, a set of even broader shoulders, equally naked, and a mustachioed face that was mottled several shades of red.

"Who the hell are you?" the mulberry bandit challenged.

2

~~~

"Who the hell are *you?*" Corey countered. She was in no mood to be hassled, especially by some naked barbarian. "And what are you doing in my mulberry tree?"

"Lady, if you're claiming that mulberry tree, then you're claiming that damned cat up there, so I'd appreciate it if you'd get him down, tie him to a brick, and drop him off the nearest bridge. Where the devil is Abigail?"

Having dealt with more than one crackpot in her years of community service, Corey knew better than to attempt to reason with the unreasonable—especially in ninety-degree heat, when tempers were already soaring. Nevertheless, she tried for a conciliatory approach. "Touch one hair on that cat's head and you'll be picking up your teeth."

"Where's Abigail?" the man repeated. Some of the

violent color was beginning to fade from his craggy face by now, throwing into dramatic relief a bushy mustache, a few scratches, and several smears of what was probably mulberry juice.

"I wouldn't think of disturbing Abbie," Corey announced coolly. "Why don't you just bug off before I lose my temper?"

Eyes the color of tarnished brass narrowed dangerously, and Corey took a step backward. The noise from next door continued unabated. "If that damned bird doesn't shut up, I'm going to slit his throat," she vowed, planting her fists on her hips.

"Reach out a hand to harm my bird and you'll draw back a nub."

"That screeching banshee is *yours?*" Astounded, Corey took in the belligerent stance, the wild sun-streaked hair, the shaggy mustache, and the rumpled undershorts. "You're *McLaughlin?*"

"So?" he shot back aggressively. "Listen, lady, if you're another one of my mother's bright ideas, then you can just trot your little carcass right back across the bridge. I don't know how the hell you tracked me down, but you're wasting your time, because I am not—repeat, *not*—interested. And you can tell my mother that when and if I decide I want a woman, I'll damned well pick out my own candidates, is that clear?"

Corey continued to stare, her mouth hanging slightly open, until McLaughlin leaned forward and lifted her chin with a square-tipped finger. When she scrubbed furiously at the place he'd touched, a look of wicked amusement flickered across his irregular features.

"I must admit though, my mother's taste is getting better all the time," he drawled thoughtfully. "You're an

25

improvement over the last one. Even she was beginning to look fairly interesting until the business with Toad and the vacuum cleaner."

A frog and a vacuum cleaner? How gruesome! Corey shuddered and made an attempt to regain the control she felt slipping away. Subjecting him to a cool, disparaging look designed to highlight the contrast between her high-fashion resort wear and his state of mulberry-stained dishabille, she said, "Aren't you a little too old to be stealing fruit from other people's trees?" He was so close that she could see the network of lines fanning out from his angry eyes. Instinctively, she adjusted his age upward from her first impression.

"I wasn't after your berries, I was trying to strangle that damned cat before Toad beat his brains out on the screen."

"Toad? I thought your toad got vacuumed up."

McLaughlin closed his eyes momentarily. "Patience, man," he muttered under his breath. Aloud, he explained slowly, "Toad is a yellow-naped Amazon—a *parrot!* He happens to be intelligent and affectionate, not to mention valuable, which is a damn sight more than I can say for that flea-ridden tomcat of Abigail's."

"It's a damn sight more than I can say for any man who'd name a parrot Frog, too," Corey snapped.

"Toad!"

"Whatever! I'm not sure if your poor mother's trying to marry you off or just find you a housekeeper, but I can certainly understand her concern; you need a keeper!"

"Well, lady, if you're applying for the job, you're flat out of luck," McLaughlin snarled. The arms crossed over his chest bore a patchwork of magenta stains and scratches, and Corey knew a moment's compunction at having been partly responsible.

"You couldn't *pay* me enough," she jeered. A trickle of perspiration found its way down the valley of her spine, and she squirmed uncomfortably. "Look, for your information, McLaughlin, I'm no more thrilled with the prospect of having a neighbor than you are. I came all the way from Missouri just to be alone here, and I don't intend to let any wild-haired hack writer keep me from it. Now, if you don't mind, I've got groceries to tend to."

McLaughlin executed a sweeping bow. "Allow me to be your first Tarheel victim. It's an honor to be ostracized by such an expert. What's the matter, did they run you out of Missouri?"

"Go to hell, McLaughlin."

"Tell Abigail to get her damned cat inside if she wants to see him in one piece again."

Corey hesitated. In all fairness, she had to accept the blame for Jack's transgressions. Abbie had spelled out the rules quite clearly. McLaughlin wrote at night, and during the morning, he did whatever a writer does when he isn't writing. He slept during the afternoon. The bird went out onto the porch while he was sleeping, and after hearing a sample of the creature's vocal accomplishments, Corey could understand why. She'd promised to keep Jack inside from one until five, and she'd forgotten.

"It's my first day," she admitted grudgingly. "I had errands to do in town and I forgot, but it won't happen again, I assure you."

"It's not up to you. Abigail and I had an agreement. That bloodthirsty throwback is her responsibility." Bare feet braced apart on the hot sand, Rune McLaughlin was beginning to regret this whole episode. He'd been sound asleep when all hell had broken loose, and he'd raced over here without even bothering to get dressed. Abigail, from what he'd learned of her during the three weeks he'd been in residence, wasn't the type to quibble over a lack of formality in an emergency.

Only instead of his landlady, he'd run into this stiff-necked female who, on the hottest day in June, could freeze a man with those ice-gray eyes of hers. Missouri or not, he'd bet his last dime that either she'd read that damned article, or *her* mother was a friend of *his* mother's. The old gal just wouldn't give up. "Who are you, anyway?" he asked, curiosity outstripping his sense of self-preservation for once.

They both started as a ball of yellow fur landed beneath the mulberry tree and streaked off toward the dunes. After one last bloodcurdling shriek from the screened porch, silence settled once more.

Corey turned back to McLaughlin. "Corey Peters. I'm Abbie's cousin." Warily, she extended her hand.

Just as warily, Rune took it, pressed once—firmly—and released it. "Visiting long?" There was nothing at all hospitable in his tone.

"A few weeks." She was beginning to suspect that her visit might extend beyond the six weeks Abbie had originally mentioned. McLaughlin obviously didn't know about Abbie's trip, and Corey considered whether or not to mention it. She decided not. Abbie's Chevy was still in its usual parking place. With her Chrysler and McLaughlin's disreputable-looking truck, the double driveway was fairly crowded.

McLaughlin nodded abruptly. "Well—sorry if I was a bit abrupt."

Corey admired the masterly understatement. "My ault," she submitted graciously. "I'll keep Jack under control from now on; you can count on it." She took another backward step. "Uh, about the swimming pool," she began hesitantly.

"It's all yours. I promised Abigail I'd take care of the maintenance for her, but when it comes to swimming, I'll ake the ocean."

"Thanks. I don't know anything about tides, currents, waves—that sort of thing, and Abbie said there's not a lifeguard for this stretch, since it isn't populated enough to warrant it."

"Right. You'll do better to paddle around in the pool." Rune tilted his head thoughtfully to study the woman before him. "You're sure you never met my mother?" Helen McLaughlin had been trying to match him up with a succession of females who carried her personal seal of approval since his prep-school days, when at eighteen, he'd unexpectedly found himself engaged to a thrice-divorced bartender.

Gravely, Corey shook her head. "Sorry to disappoint you, but I never heard of you before Abbie told me she had a tenant. As for your mother, until you mentioned her, I thought you must have been incubated in a heap of rotting vegetation on the banks of a Florida swamp."

A gleam of appreciation danced across the metallic surface of Rune's eyes as he caught the reptilian reference. "Yeah, well . . . just so you don't try to hypnotize me by stroking my belly."

"You've already warned me, thanks. I assure you, I don't want to draw back a nub, as you so poetically put it."

Unbidden, Corey's eyes dropped to his unclad middle,

and her fingers curled defensively into her palms. Sweat trickled down his deeply tanned flesh and clung to the flattened curls that trailed from the thatch on his chest to disappear under the elastic waistband. With each breath he took, the merciless sun set scores of salty prisms dancing.

Earlier, she'd set his age at somewhere in the mid-thirties. Then she'd revised it upward several years. Now she was beginning to wonder if her first estimate hadn't been the correct one. For a writer who kept abominable hours, he was surprisingly fit.

At the sound of the deep laughter, she lifted her head to glare at him.

"Seen enough, or do you want the back view, too? The buns don't show to their best advantage in this outfit, I'm afraid." He flexed a set of creditable biceps and grinned under the shaggy mustache, and Corey came to a quiet boil. Damn it, he'd been watching *her* watching *him!*

"I just wanted to be sure I'd recognize your picture the next time I go to the post office," she said sweetly as she wheeled away to deal with her melting groceries. Cat scratches, mulberry stains, and all, he was completely out of her league. She'd do well to stay clear of him.

It turned out to be no problem. For the next few days, all Corey saw of her contentious neighbor was a set of footprints on the beach. She walked before breakfast, and evidently McLaughlin did, too. His footprints crossed the dune and invariably veered southward; she turned to the north, and an unspoken agreement seemed to have been struck.

She walked at sunup, and again just after the sun went down. In between, she read and ate and experimented with makeup. She took the sun in easy stages during the afternoons while McLaughlin slept, oiling her body and working her way from a relatively modest one-piece to the string bikini she'd bought especially for sunning.

When the water in the swimming pool cooled down at night, she swam short laps and then floated while her mind drifted over half a dozen nebulous career possibilities. Later, playing the hair dryer impatiently over her long, thick hair, she worked on convincing herself to have it cut short. After wearing it long all her life, the decision wasn't as easy as she'd thought it was going to be. What if she got herself shorn and then decided she didn't like it?

Searching through Abbie's extensive library, she came across a shell book. After that, she began paying more attention to the specimens she found on her daily walks. She'd already amassed a small collection, and instead of dumping them on Abbie's porch, she began arranging them in a whimsical mosaic on the landward side of the dune.

And she slept. Oh, heavens, how she slept! With the ceiling fan wafting softly overhead and the muted roar of the ocean just outside her window, she was asleep by nine and awake by daybreak, feeling incredibly refreshed. It was as though she'd thrown open the windows of her soul and let the healing sea breezes blow away the chaff of the past.

After pulling on one of the more practical items she'd bought on her St. Louis binge, a white cotton gauze jumpsuit, she rolled up the sleeves above the elbow, and the legs to just below her knee, taking time to admire her pale coppery tan. It didn't quite cover her whole body yet, but there was plenty of time. While there was certainly no reason to believe that McLaughlin was interested in watching a thirty-seven-year-old woman bare her all to the sun, she'd discovered that she was still too self-conscious to do more than loosen her straps while she lay on her stomach.

Snatching an apple, she let herself out the door and called softly to Jack. He'd taken to accompanying her for the first hundred yards or so, at which point he'd sit on the dune with a disdainful look on his broad face and wait to ambush her on her return.

The surf was crystal-clear, with a lazy fringe of suds that invited her to play tag. Holding her half-eaten apple above the salt spray, she flung herself into the game, darting toward the water and retreating as the waves threatened. Sooner or later she was going to work up her nerve to try ocean swimming. Maybe she could walk half a mile or so to the motel beach. There was a lifeguard there, and always several swimmers. Her swimming was adequate, if nothing spectacular, but in spite of sporadic bursts of bravado, she was still feeling a bit too vulnerable to tackle anything so vast.

Jack was waiting for her, although he pretended to ignore her approach. A few feet beyond him there was a neat stack of perfect cockleshells. "Jack, you old scoundrel, you shouldn't have," Corey crowed, gathering them up against her damp and sandy bosom.

Ignoring her, the tomcat extended a hind leg and commenced grooming himself, and she lifted her eyes to the uncompromising lines of her neighbor's cottage. The blank stare of the screens offered no clue, but of course it had to have been McLaughlin. A friendly overture? Hardly. He'd probably picked up the things and then decided he didn't want them. What was more natural than to dump them before he crossed the dune?

Nevertheless, when she returned from her evening walk, Corey found another small heap of shells waiting for her. Thoughtfully, she gathered them up, rinsed them with the hose, and began incorporating them into her shell mosaic, a fantasy landscape complete with a toad-like creature and a winged serpent.

By the end of her first full week, Corey had begun to relax her guard. Whoever or whatever McLaughlin was, he was evidently as serious about wanting privacy as she was. Was he a published writer? Did he write fiction or nonfiction? Judging from appearances alone, she suspected he wrote bad novels of the counterculture variety. And judging from the looks of his truck, he was either still unpublished or a resounding flop.

"Which might explain his rotten disposition," she muttered, clutching her bra to her as she stood up to straighten her rumpled beach towel. Sunning was harder work than she'd suspected. She'd much rather be inside under the fan, finishing the book she'd started last night.

With the north side of McLaughlin's cottage overlooking the pool, there was no way she could completely dismiss him from her thoughts for long. As irrational as it was, Corey found herself worrying about him. For a man his age to be living a hand-to-mouth existence while he tried to make a living as a writer was somehow pathetic.

At least she had the solace of knowing she'd been an excellent wife, a capable manager, and a good mother, she told herself, smiling at the irony. She might be sliding rapidly into middle age and grandmotherhood, husbandless, and with a daughter who preferred to "do it herself," but at least she knew her own worth.

"Oh, blast," Corey muttered in self-disgust. She'd promised herself to leave all that west of the Mississippi. Rolling over onto her back, she tossed aside her bra and exposed her bare breasts, slightly shocked at the sensual feelings aroused by the burning kiss of the sun on a formerly unkissed area. Edwin had been an athletic, but unimaginative lover. He'd been unfaithful almost from the first. Corey had sensed the difference, although she hadn't known the cause at first. She'd put it down to her pregnancy, and later to the demands of a nursing infant.

Saint Corey, Abbie had called her, but God, she'd had to do something. Ed was never home, and once Winnie was in school, she'd had to drown her anxiety in *something*. There were worse ways to go than community service.

The smell of chlorine drifted up to her nostrils, and she turned her head away from the pool. Her gaze lifted to the screened windows of McLaughlin's cottage, and she wondered idly when he did his pool maintenance. She'd never seen him there, but then, they were both pretty expert at avoiding each other.

A thought occurred to her. She tried to dismiss it, but it refused to dislodge. What if he were really needy? Unless he happened to write a runaway best-seller, he might have trouble making ends meet between books, and no best-selling author she'd ever heard of lived in a squatty gray rental cottage and drove a rusty pickup truck.

Oh Lord, what if he were actually *hungry?* Corey's

social conscience rose to smite her. How long could she go on cooking three meals a day for one, knowing that right next door there was a starving man? He'd swapped his labor for the roof over his head, and it must have cost him dearly to have to bargain for that much. Men had so much pride about that sort of thing.

Abbie, of course, would be a pushover. She had a romantic streak a mile wide, and some down-on-his-luck hack who looked like a cross between Tom Selleck and Edgar Allan Poe would have been able to break through her crust in a minute.

Corey stroked another layer of oil into her pale breasts, spreading the excess down her flat stomach. It was none of her business. If he was really hard up, she certainly didn't begrudge him a roof over his head. As for what he ate . . .

What *did* he eat? He never seemed to go anywhere, either to shop or to eat out. As far as she could tell, his truck hadn't moved since the day she'd arrived. It just sat there collecting rust, dust, and mulberry-colored droppings. If he fished, she'd seen no evidence of it. She wouldn't object to picking up a few items from the grocers, if he asked her. She was sorry now that she'd chased him out of the mulberry tree. He'd claimed to be after Jack, but that might have been just an excuse to save face.

Lifting her head, Corey squinted in an attempt to judge the shade of her doneness. She'd dozed on her stomach before rolling over, and now the tender flesh of her back registered every wrinkle in the beach towel. If she got herself blistered, there'd be no one around to anoint the spots she couldn't reach. Unless she cared to go next door with a bottle of burn lotion and beg a helping hand. McLaughlin and his paranoia would have a field day with that.

On Saturday morning Corey walked as usual. The rising sun hid its fire behind a veil of low clouds as she scuffed the suds on the way back to the cottage. Should she call Winnie again so soon or wait a few days? She'd talked to her the day after she'd arrived at Emerald Isle, and she'd detected a definite tone of relief when she'd hinted that she might be staying longer than six weeks.

"Mother, what on earth will you do in Morristown? Maybe you could get a job in St. Louis or somewhere, but you know what this place's like. There's just nothing to do. Maybe Daddy could find you something at the store, but where would you live now that you've sold the house?"

In other words, Corey had interpreted, tears constricting her throat, there wouldn't be room in a two-bedroom bungalow in River Hill for three adults. As if she'd even consider moving in with them!

"Actually, I thought I might look around this neck of the woods as long as I'm here. Tourism is the big thing, and I figure the sum total of my past experience should fit me to run a major hotel single-handed, what do you think?"

Winnie had laughed at that, and the relief had been obvious. Corey had reminded herself of how it had been when she'd been newly married and fiercely independent. Some things didn't change from generation to generation.

She sighed as a wave caught her, soaking her to the waist. The gauze jumpsuit would dry quickly enough, and she splashed through the incoming tide heedlessly, still caught up in the small town she'd so recently escaped and the angry scene of two months earlier. She'd been ruthlessly weeding out an eighteen-year accumulation of old photographs when Mike and Winnie had confronted her with the news that Winnie was pregnant.

Mike had broken it. "Mrs. Peters, Winnie and I are pregnant," he'd said, his good-looking face painfully red.

"And we're going to be married, no matter what you say," Winnie had added.

Corey had taken it badly. Coming so close on top of her divorce, it had been too much. She'd felt betrayed, deserted, and she'd let it all out. Mike and Winnie had listened to everything she'd had to say, hands clutching tightly, misery in the set of their eyes, their young mouths, but in the end, nothing had changed.

From that day on, Corey had done her best to treat Mike as though he were her son, and Winnie as though she were a dear and respected friend instead of a seventeen-year-old daughter who was probably making the biggest single mistake in her life.

Blindly retracing the sea-washed trail of her own footprints, Corey comforted herself with the thought that she'd finally found the grace to accept the inevitable. She'd apologized to them both, and then she'd set about giving them the best wedding she could arrange at short notice. Not until they were on their honeymoon, and the last of the rice had been swept away, leaving the house ready for the realtor to begin showing, did Corey take time to consider the situation from her own personal perspective.

That was when panic had set in. Cruise literature had been sent for and then discarded unread; she'd called a local spa and then changed her mind about joining. Lists had been started and crumpled, lists of assets and liabilities, both personal and financial. She'd called Abbie and talked for hours, and then called again when the initial desperation had begun to ebb.

"'Morning, Ms. Peters."

Startled, Corey looked up to see McLaughlin seated on the top of the dune. "Good morning, Mr. McLaughlin." He'd obviously been swimming. His hair, shaggier than ever, was wet and standing on end, but at least the black boxers he wore were the swimming variety this time.

"I found something I think you can use." Reaching behind him, Rune produced a perfect pen shell, both sides intact and still hinged. "Don't think I've ever seen one in this good condition before. Thought it might be just the thing for your pterodactyl."

He made a genuine effort to lift his eyes from her body to her face, and failed. Lordy, she was a sight to behold in those see-through pajama things. She probably had no idea of how transparent they were when they were wet.

On the other hand, maybe she did. Maybe that was part of her plan.

What the devil, so she was probably just another avaricious lady who'd read that detestable Ten Most Eligible article and decided to cast her bait in his direction and see what she could reel in. At thirty-nine, he was certainly experienced enough to enjoy a little of what he'd been missing lately without getting himself hooked.

"What do you think?" he asked with a nod at the shell she was examining. "Too small?"

"It's perfect," Corey murmured, examining the fan-shaped bivalve. "I'm amazed you recognized my ptero-dactyl. I can't seem to make it look like anything but a chicken."

"It's all in the beak. Try a razor clam curved down-ward. Uh—how was the water?"

"The water?" Following his glance, Corey groaned and turned away, wrapping her arms around her. "Why didn't you tell me?"

"Considering the way I was dressed for our first meeting, I think we're past standing on ceremony, don't you, Ms. Peters?"

"It's Corey, and if you don't mind, I'll go put on a shirt."

With deceptive ease, McLaughlin unfolded himself and stood, and Corey was acutely aware of the sheer physical presence of the man. In fact, it had been years since she'd been so aware of that inexplicable magnetism an attract-ive man could exert.

"Sure thing," he said genially. "See you around then, Corey."

Bare feet digging into the warm sand, Corey waited until the unexpected surge of disappointment had spent itself, and then she plodded down the back side of the dune and into her cottage. She'd only meant to dash in and grab something to cover up with, for Pete's sake! He didn't have to leave.

Under the cottage, tucked away in a catchall storage room, Corey discovered a rusty grill. With a lot of scouring and the strategic use of foil, she finally pro-nounced it ready for use. She had one T-bone steak left, a can of mushrooms, and a few fresh vegetables for a salad. A baked potato would have been nice, but she wasn't about to heat up the house with the oven just for one tiny potato.

After lunch, she shut Jack in the house for his afternoon nap and drove to the post office to mail a letter to the children. On the way back, she picked up a bag of charcoal, a pint of starter fluid, and a jug of modestly priced imported red wine. It sounded vaguely familiar; she only hoped it wouldn't be too caustic. If she was going to broaden her experience, there was no time like the present.

Just as the sun disappeared behind the wind-sculpted vegetation on the sound side of the barrier island, Corey dragged the grill to the top of the dune and dumped in charcoal with a lavish hand. Fire building and grilling had always been Edwin's job; everything else, including the monumental job of cleaning up afterward, hers.

After dousing the coals generously with fluid, she struck a match, only to have it go out immediately. She tried another one, and another. Glaring at the growing heap of black-tipped kindling around the base of the grill, she swore succinctly. She had exactly three more kitchen matches. If those didn't work, she'd fry the damned thing!

"Need a hand?"

At the smooth baritone interruption, Corey spun around. "Do you have a lighter? Matches just don't work. I don't understand it. I could do better than this rubbing two sticks together."

Rune glanced at the jumble of burned matchsticks on the ground. His gaze encompassed her bare feet and moved up her long honey-colored legs. It was coming right along, that tan of hers. God knows, he wished she'd get done and call it quits. She'd thrown his whole schedule off.

His hand closed over hers and he removed the box of kitchen matches. Next he rearranged the charcoal, and then he extracted a single match. Cupping his hands, he struck it, shielding the flame until he'd touched the coal in several places.

"You must have used a gallon of fluid," he observed wryly. "Whatever you're planning to grill is going to pick up the taste. What kind of wood chips are you using?"

Wood chips. Ed had used something in a box that had to be soaked in water first; the ritual had taken ages. "I forgot to buy any."

"No problem." Rune turned away and jogged out to the highway. Glancing in both directions, he crossed and quickly disappeared into the dense scrub that sloped down to Bogue Sound.

Corey waited, growing more and more uncomfortable. The least she could do after all his help was invite him to share, but one tiny T-bone and a salad wasn't much to share.

She watched him trot back up the driveway brandishing a small branch. He had none of the knotted massiveness of the superjocks Ed so admired. His legs were those of a runner, the breadth of his shoulders nicely counterpointed by lean hips and a narrow, flat waist. He was in the black trunks again. Late-day sunshine glinted on the furring that patterned his chest and arrowed downward.

Maybe that was all he had to wear. Oh, no, she thought distraughtly, the man *couldn't* be that broke, no matter how bad a writer he was. He was certainly able-bodied enough; if he were really desperate, he could always find a job doing something.

"Myrtle," Rune announced. "Tastes a lot like bay, but spicier. I'll chop it and soak it for you, and you can add some on just before you get ready to cook—which won't be anytime this week, from the looks of those flames."

"Too much, huh? I thought I might get my evening walk in while I waited for it to burn down."

"Sounds good. I'm a little late with my evening constitutional, too. Toad's molting, and I had to clean the feathers out of my typewriter, and one thing led to another." Without too much trouble, he located a rusty hatchet in Abbie's storage room and began chipping off slivers of the green wood. "Want to fill the bucket with water for me? They should be ready by the time your fire's under control."

Rune swung into step with her as comfortably as if they'd been walking together every day instead of conscientiously avoiding each other. Neither of them spoke. Corey walked as close to the water's edge as she could, casting frequent sidelong glances at her companion. With a haircut and some decent clothes, he'd be terrific. The mustache was still shaggy, but he'd obviously trimmed it since she'd seen him last. He had an effortless way of walking that pleased her immensely. In fact, with a little practice, and perhaps a pair of dark glasses, she might turn into a fairly competent man-watcher.

Not beefcake, though, she was disenchanted with all that brawn. She knew exactly how much beef and beer and milk it took to build all those muscles, because she'd seen her month's food budget wrecked again and again when Ed had casually invited his football friends to move in for as long as they wanted to. She was about as antijock as anyone could be whose livelihood depended on the sales of sporting goods.

Had depended. Past tense. She'd kept the house, because she'd darned well earned something besides room and board for her eighteen years, but she'd refused to accept alimony. After the mortgage was paid off with the proceeds from the sale, the rest would be invested for the children. She'd have to find some way to support herself, but at the moment she was enjoying the first vacation she'd had in eighteen years that didn't involve some sporting event.

They walked for perhaps a mile, and then, by mutual consent, turned back. The sun had long since set, and in the afterglow, the pale light of a near-full moon began to brighten the eastern horizon.

"Look at that lovely, pearly glow. I don't think I've ever known such a complete sense of peacefulness," Corey said softly.

"The imprisoned splendor."

Without breaking her easy stride, Corey glanced at him. "That's got to be a quote, but I haven't the foggiest notion of what it's from."

" 'Paracelsus.' "

"I don't suppose you'd care to elaborate? Morristown Community College seems to have had a few gaps in its curriculum."

"I never discuss literature on an empty stomach—or on a first date."

"This is a date?" Corey scoffed. She waded blithely through an incoming wave.

"With a little manipulation, I don't see why we can't

43

turn it into one. For instance, I could bring a donation from my kitchen and join you for a potluck dinner."

Corey felt a shiver of delicious excitement race through her. "My grill or yours?" she tossed off playfully. Not bad for someone who's been sidelined as long as I have, she congratulated herself.

3

Afterward, Corey was never quite sure how it had come about, that cease-fire of theirs. Rune had produced two enormous, perfectly baked potatos, compliments of his microwave oven, and after one glance at the wine she'd bought, he'd trotted back to his own kitchen and returned with something more to his own taste.

"Sorry," Corey apologized, shoving her jug of Spanish red behind a chair. "I have this list of things I'm going to accomplish this summer, a sort of C. M. Peters reconstruction plan, you know? Part two, subheading A is to learn something about wines. Nothing pretentious, mind you, just enough so that I don't inadvertently insult my guests."

Rune wielded a corkscrew with commendable efficiency. "If by guest, you mean me, Corey, then forget it. I'm just a cranky neighbor with a low tolerance for silent suffering. But tell me more about this reconstruction project of yours. Offhand, I'd say you wouldn't need a very long list."

"Twenty-two inches."

"Twenty-two inches?" He shot her a puzzled look.

"Two eight-and-a-half-by-eleven inch sheets." And as he continued to stare at her, she exclaimed, "My *list!* Of improvements. Maybe you'd better get started on your own list. Item one, work on your memory."

Rune nodded thoughtfully. "Come to think of it, I guess I'm embarked on something of the sort myself. What would you say to a mutual aid agreement?"

"That depends. Which are you going to work on first, temper or memory?"

The corners of a grin disappeared under cover of his luxurious, sun-streaked mustache. "Temper? What makes you think I have a temper?"

"See? I told you your memory was lousy. What was that you were threatening me with a few days ago, something about drawing back a nub?"

"Just kidding, honest. Go ahead, test me—stroke my belly, and I'll purr like Abigail's tomcat."

"Just about," Corey retorted dryly, recalling Jack's uncertain disposition.

"Now, what do you want to know about part two, subheading A?"

"Part two, subheading what?" It was Corey's turn to be puzzled.

"And you think *I've* got a problem with memory? Wines, woman—wines!"

"I was only testing you. Hmmm, wines," she repeated

thoughtfully. "I don't even know what I *don't* know. When your father's a Methodist minister and you're married right out of high school to a devout beer drinker, you don't fool around much with wines. I've stuck with the house white for years, but once, a friend tried to get me to try an ingenuous—honestly, that was what she called it—an ingenuous little rosé with just a kiss of impertinence."

"After prose like that, you probably needed a double shot of Pepto-Bismol. However, I do happen to have a modest, unassuming little beer, if you'd rather have it."

"You're too kind," Corey mocked. "In Morristown, the men drink beer and the wives drink the house white. It's an unwritten rule. Except for two extremely sophisticated women from St. Louis who opened up a health spa last fall. They always order Perrier with a twist of lime."

"God save the queen," Rune said reverently. "I think we can do better than that. Like limeade? I'll lay in some supplies and we'll start you off on margaritas, and then work our way through a few of the classics—martini, Tom Collins—in due time we'll arrive at a civilized summer drink like gin and tonic."

Lips twitching with suppressed laughter, Corey said, "After all that, I won't even be able to *find* my list, much less read it. What about your own reconstruction project? Can't I return the favor?" Her gaze touched briefly on his shaggy head of hair and his less than formal attire. When it came to offering grooming hints, she'd have to tread carefully; Rune struck her as a man with rather more pride than he could afford, under the circumstances.

So she was married, Rune mused. No rings in evidence, but if he'd looked closer, he'd have noticed the smooth indentation on her third finger, left hand. His grin faded slowly as he leaned back in Abigail's sagging rocker. They'd moved the impromptu dinner party inside when the mosquitoes had descended. "We'll have to compare lists one of these days, but I doubt if mine's half as interesting as yours. So what's this husband of yours doing while you broaden your experience here on the East Coast?"

"Setting up house with his new wife, probably."

"Ouch. Did I hit a nerve?" It might pay to proceed with caution. If he proceeded at all.

"No," Corey replied simply. That particular nerve had healed. There were others, though, that were still too raw for comfort.

Rune raked a hand through his hair, feeling the stickiness of salt. He should have taken time to shower and change after his last swim, but it had been a case of grabbing the moment and running with it. She was an enigma, all right, this divorced daughter of a Methodist preacher from Missouri—a woman who closed her eyes, parted her lips, and bared her breasts to the sun, only to race for a cover-up the first time he caught her in a wet jumpsuit. What sort of woman carried herself with such an inherent air of pride, wore clothes of the quality she wore, and still didn't know any better than to bring home a jug of cheap rotgut? There seemed to be a few discrepancies here.

"So Abigail's gone gallivanting." He deemed it politic to change the subject. "Are you actually a cousin, or was that just something you thought up on the spur of the moment?"

Corey squeezed both ends of her potato to allow the steam to escape. She'd meticulously divided her steak, doubled the salad, and added lots of cheese. With Rune's potatoes, there was plenty for both of them.

"We're first cousins," she stated. "Abbie's father was much older than mine, but Abbie and I have always been close." As an afterthought, she asked, "Why should I lie about it?"

If he mentioned the article, he'd have to explain it, and if she really hadn't seen it, there was no point in setting himself up. "I told you, I thought my mother had put you on my trail."

"To do what?" The steak was well done, just as she liked it. The myrtle lent an intriguing touch, and Corey cut off another bit of the tenderloin.

Rune concentrated on slicing his leathery meat from the bone. Next time, he'd do the cooking. He glanced up with a guileless smile. "To get me into a compromising position so I'd have to marry you."

The bite of tenderloin went down the wrong way, and by the time Corey had caught her breath again, she could almost admire his gall. "You know, for a would-be writer who makes his living servicing swimming pools, you have a pretty healthy ego. Why would I go to such lengths to entrap you?"

He shrugged, and Corey's gaze was drawn to the play of lamplight on the satiny skin of his bare shoulders. "Offhand, I can't think of a single reason," he said carelessly, "but you know mothers. Mine has this big thing about leaving me alone and unprotected when she shuffles off this mortal coil."

Corey leaned forward, her eyes softening with concern. "Your mother's ill?"

"Ill? Hell no. Healthy as an ox. Garden club, historical society, symphony guild, board of education—you name it, she's in it up to her pearl-studded ears. She's just afraid I'll get tangled up with a woman who's—to use her own phrase—not our kind of people."

Corey's gaze strayed to the unkempt thatch of sun-streaked brown hair. Something was decidedly out of kilter here. Two and two were adding up to three. "You're a black sheep!" she pronounced as certain things fell into place. "I should have guessed. You came from a decent, respectable home, and now you've dropped out to be the sort of writer who tries to discredit the very society that produced him." There was no way she could keep the disapproval from her voice.

"You're convicting me on some pretty flimsy evidence," Rune accused. With the expertise of long practice, he sifted through the facts and selected a few of the more innocuous ones. "I haven't dropped out of anything. My father and I were best friends till the day he died, and my mother and I are still on excellent terms. In all but one area, that is. She deplores my taste in women, and I'm appalled at hers."

"If you say so," Corey allowed dubiously. "But what I can't figure out is whether she's trying to find you a woman or save you from one."

Rune examined the clean bone on his plate and then turned regretfully to his unfinished salad. "Both. That's what makes it so tricky. She's afraid her only son's going to be snapped up by some . . . uh," he bit back the word *gold digger* just in time. "Some wealthy, decadent female to end his days as a glorified gigolo. Her favorite tactic is the surprise inspection." He grimaced comically. "And her favorite time to come calling is between seven and nine on a weekend morning. As a backup plan, she keeps dredging up these depressingly nice women and arranging for me to trip over them."

"Speaking as a former depressingly nice woman, I assure you, I'll stay well clear of your feet." It was a joke, but Corey found that she wasn't particularly amused.

"Oh, hell, honey, nothing personal, but after managing to stay clear of entanglements for thirty-nine years, what would I want with a wife now?"

"More to the point, what would a wife want with *you?*" Corey shot back.

"Exactly." Rune cursed his own tactlessness. Without knowing the circumstances of her divorce, he might be treading on a mine field. "Look, all I meant was that a bachelor can get along just fine these days, what with fancy frozen dishes and drip-dry clothes."

"If you own any clothes, it's news to me," Corey snorted. For a moment there the joke had threatened to get out of hand. This was unfamiliar territory, the half-flirtatious give-and-take between a man and a woman. And she was almost twenty years out of practice.

"One thing about being your own boss, you can set your own dress code." It occurred to Rune that his toplessness didn't bother her nearly as much as hers had him. Of course, if he'd been any sort of a gentleman, he wouldn't have looked, but since the first day, when he'd happened to see her oiling down that long beautifully constructed body of hers, he'd found one excuse after another to be near the north gable shortly after lunch.

"So . . . what do when you're not beachcombing or working on your suntan, Corey Peters? Are you a schoolteacher, too?"

Tilting her glass, Corey concentrated on capturing the

flicker of lamplight through the ruby liquid. "I love this color," she murmured.

"Offhand, I can't think of too many occupations that offer a six-week vacation," Rune persisted. It was none of his business. As a lawyer, he knew that better than most. As a lawyer, he'd also seen his share of men stripped to the bone by some greedy little piranha. Somehow, though, he was pretty sure that Corey Peters's ex-husband wasn't among them. And, of course, it was possible that she really had no knowledge of his background, either professional or social. Or financial. But when a man had been a target all his life, he learned to duck first and ask questions later.

"Do all writers ask so many questions?"

Maybe he'd better duck again. "Writers have all sorts of little-known privileges."

"Writers also have more nerve than the law allows." Corey laughed at his unsuccessful attempt to look remorseful. "My turn now. What sort of things do you write, Rune? Confessions? Technical tomes? Should I have heard of you, by the way?"

"I doubt it. Now that you've finally convinced me that you're not another one of my mother's—"

"Depressingly nice women?" she finished for him. "For the last time, Rune, I've never *heard* of your mother. Personally, I think you need to get help for that Oedipus complex of yours—or is it plain old garden-variety paranoia?"

Rune watched the shadow of her long lashes dance across her eyes as she teased him. She was turning out to be unexpectedly good company. There was a certain subtlety about her that appealed to him enormously, like the Victorian house his grandparents had lived in when he was a kid. He'd never tired of exploring it, for there was always some new aspect to capture his imagination.

"What do you write, Rune? Westerns? Spy thrillers? Cops and robbers?"

"What makes you so sure I don't write the heavy sort of stuff that everyone claims to have read, but nobody actually reads?"

Chasing the last sliver of mushroom around her salad bowl, Corey gave the question serious consideration. "I'm not sure," she said, munching thoughtfully. "I think it's the bird. No man who'd name a helpless parrot Toad could possibly write anything of any great social significance."

"Helpless parrot, my bare—foot," Rune responded with outrage. "His name was Prince when I bought him. He was barely feathered out, but let me tell you, no critter who can inflict so much pain with such a variety of sharp instruments is worthy of coronation. I gave him two months to straighten out. He didn't, so I rechristened him. We accept each other's failings now, and get along just fine."

Rune reached for the bottle and divided what was left of the wine between their two glasses. "I shouldn't," Corey murmured, watching greedily as the last drop was poured. "It's not at all sour. Write it down for me, will you? I'll look for it next time I go to the grocery store."

"I'll send over a few bottles," Rune offered. He saw no point in mentioning that his favorite wine dealer had bought all the available stock for a few select customers.

"Oh, but I couldn't allow you to—"

"Of course you could. Now, bring on that twenty-two-inch list you mentioned. Shall we tackle another project?"

Corey's laughter mingled with the muted soughing of the surf. "Actually, I write large, so the length isn't all that relevant. Anyhow, it's your turn next. Let's see now, what could there possibly be about you that could stand improvement?"

"At least I don't cut my friends to ribbons with sarcasm," he informed her piously.

"Speaking of cutting, I used to trim the shaggy dogs for the animal shelter when we were sprucing them up for adoption."

At his bark of laughter, Corey grimaced. "Oops, I didn't really mean that the way it came out. It must be the wine. I'm not usually quite so tactless, honestly."

"You're forgiven." Under salt-caked eyebrows, Rune's eyes were glittering with amusement.

"Shall I back out before I do any more damage to your ego?"

"Barge ahead," Rune invited with a genial gesture.

"Well, what do I know about men's haircuts, anyway? Here at the beach . . ." She shrugged helplessly. "You see, back in Missouri—"

Rune howled again. Even at the risk of embarrassing her further, he simply couldn't hold it in. Bless her tender little heart, if only she knew that she was talking to the ultimate in conservativism, from the time he'd graduated from Yale Law School and gone into partnership with his father, until the time one month ago when he'd finally rebelled and taken the summer off to see, once and for all, if he had it in him to write a decent piece of science fantasy.

Of course, that damned magazine feature on the southeast's ten most eligible bachelors had been the last straw. It was all his mother's doing, complete with pictures and even a list of his favorite foods. It wasn't the first time he'd been included in one of those adolescent, asinine lists, but somehow, this one was different. Or maybe women were just more aggressive these days. Before he'd even read the thing he'd been up to his ears in bouillabaise and Grand Marnier soufflé, the dishes his mother claimed he found irresistible.

"Well, I don't see what's all *that* funny. I was only trying to be helpful, you know. What if your editor or publisher, or whoever it is you deal with, should suddenly ask you out to lunch? Would you go in what you happened to be wearing at the moment?"

Rune sobered. Reaching across the table, he laid his hand over hers. "Honey, I hate to disillusion you still further, but at this point, I don't have an editor or a publisher or even an agent. As much as I hate to admit it, all I have at this point is sixty-seven double-spaced pages of indifferent science fantasy and one hell of a writer's block."

Her hand was burning under the weight of his palm. Valiantly, Corey tried to summon a measure of sympathy, but she was far too aware of the man across the table from her. He might as well be nude. From where she sat, all she could see was the pelt on his chest, those gleaming shoulders, and a set of irregular features that somehow worked together to form an unbelievably attractive whole —in spite of all that shaggy hair.

Rune's eyes captured hers and held them with a force she found mildly hypnotic. "Corey? Thank you, darling. Thanks for caring."

"I don't know what sort of game you're playing now," Corey mumbled, snatching her hand away, "but I've got to get these dishes washed."

It must be the wine. It had to be the wine! She wasn't the sort to get all hot and bothered over some shaggy-headed dropout with a sexy smile. Good Lord, she was going to be a grandmother!

"Why don't we leave these things until later and go for a walk on the beach? The moon's about one round shy of being full, but it ought to be rising any minute now. Have you ever been swimming in the moonlight, Corey Peters?"

"I don't swim in the ocean."

"We'll add it to your list, hmmm?"

Reaching hurriedly across the table for his wineglass, Corey knocked over the saltshaker and swore under her breath. Help, she was falling apart!

"Spilling salt's supposed to bring seven years of bad luck. Lucky for you, I happen to know the antidote." He moved around the table to stand before her, his bare feet silent on the worn wooden floors.

"That's breaking mirrors. Would you please move and let me get by?"

"Go swimming with me, my sweet, semireconstructed Corey?" Rune tempted softly.

"For the last time, I don't swim in the ocean," Corey snapped. "And would you stop all this reconstructed business? I'm sorry I ever mentioned it!"

"You're all upset because you spilled the salt," he crooned sympathetically. "I told you, darling, you have nothing to worry about."

"I'm not your darling, and it didn't spill! The shaker's clogged solid. Now, will you please—"

"I've got a cure for both those complaints, too."

She felt herself wavering. "The first is *not* a complaint, but if you can cure the clog, then speak up," she ordered,

56

trying desperately to hold out against the contagious laughter in his eyes.

"It's not half as interesting as the antidote for the other two complaints, but if you insist."

She had to laugh. Never in her life had she met a man like Rune McLaughlin. She'd been the product of a life-is-grim, life-is-serious girlhood, and then all too soon, she'd been a twenty-year-old mother with a twenty-seven-year-old husband who resented being tied down. In the constant struggle to make ends meet, there'd been too little to laugh about.

"All right, all right, go ahead and broaden my education!" she invited rashly. "And then you can get on with your jogging or swimming or whatever you have to do before you can settle down to writing again. Who knows," she cried, flinging out her arms, "maybe I can come up with an incantation that will break your writer's block."

"I'd be forever in your debt," Rune said reverently. "Would you care to incant first?"

Shaking her head in mock despair, Corey wiped her hands on the seat of her jumpsuit and lifted them, placing one on his forehead and one on the back of his head. It was all she could do to keep her fingers from threading through the thick curly strands.

Rune watched her expectantly, his eyes glowing like sulfur flames. "It's a silent incantation?"

"I'm thinking, I'm thinking!"

"Why don't I go first, then?" He stepped closer, and before Corey could retrieve her hands, he'd slipped his arms around her back and brought her close against his warm, hard body. It was incredible, the effect the touch of another human being could have on a woman. That instantaneous hammering awareness that she'd first felt at fifteen and last felt on her honeymoon, had matured into something truly awesome. Her hands braced against his warm, satiny shoulders, and she stared, mesmerized, into his eyes.

"Put rice in your shakers," Rune whispered, closing the distance she'd instinctively tried to create between them.

"My shakers?"

"Your saltshakers." His breath was having the strangest effect on her nerves, and Corey caught her bottom lip between her teeth. "Preferably uncooked rice," he murmured, with the same devastating results. "Now, about that antidote . . ."

"I'm afraid to ask," Corey gasped weakly.

"It's simple, really; you just kiss someone before the pattern of the grains is disturbed. That way, it reverses the polarity of the curse."

His face was so close she could see the fine lines around his eyes, the mossy streaks in the gold of his eyes. "You made that up," she accused.

Something was happening to her, something completely unexpected, and she wasn't at all certain she knew how to handle it.

"Would I lie to you? My nearest neighbor, my friend, if not my darling? Corey, in case a few grains accidentally got spilled when I salted my steak, I think we'd better—"

The brush of his mustache came first, and then the stunning touch of his lips. Sheer panic had her pulling back, and he whispered against her mouth, "No, Corey, no, baby—it's all right, you'll see." His hands began a slow, sensuous movement on her back, one that was probably meant to be soothing.

Corey could have told him that *soothing* was the very last word she'd ever have used to describe his touch, his taste, his scent. It was electrifying. It was intoxicating. When his tongue engaged hers, she found herself meeting each thrust eagerly. When one of his hands moved around and began to slide the thin cotton over her midsection, the tips of his thumbs brushing against the underside of her breasts, she felt a flush that started at the soles of her feet and crept upward.

His own response was unmistakable. Bracing his back against a porch support, Rune spread his feet apart and fit her intimately between his thighs, and Corey moaned softly. For one long moment more she allowed herself to float free on wave after wave of rising desire. It had been so long. She'd forgotten the driving compulsiveness that could arise so swiftly and unexpectedly. This was the same wild sweetness that had hurtled her into marriage at nineteen . . . so deceptive, so ephemeral.

And it didn't make sense, not with a perfect stranger. Alarmed at the strength of her own need, Corey began to struggle.

Rune released her almost immediately. His eyes searched her face for a clue. She'd been delightfully responsive, tasting of his wine and a subtle fresh sweetness that was hers alone. For a single instant, he'd caught a glimpse of Corey the sun-worshiper, and then something had happened and she'd raced for cover.

Still holding her fingers in his, he watched her through narrowed eyes. "Corey? What is it, honey? I won't push you too fast, don't you know that?"

"I know that, Rune." Her voice was husky as she evaded his searching gaze. "No I don't!" she cried in immediate retraction. "I don't really know you at all. Oh,

59

Rune, stop trying to confuse me." Jerking her fingers from his, she massaged her hands, turning away to stare out through the screen at the muted moonglow on the eastern horizon. "Look, could we just forget this ever happened? I'm embarrassed, if you must know, because I honestly don't know how to act in a situation like this."

"Act any way you feel like acting." Rune moved imperceptibly to a position that allowed him a clearer view of her flawless profile.

Eyes still on the nacreous scene outside, Corey laughed harshly. "That's the most irresponsible advice I think I've ever heard, Rune. Look, I really do need to get those dishes in soak." Dishes she could cope with. Congealed tallow, tarnished silver, crusted grills—those were things she could count on to remain the same, no matter whether she was married or single, young or old.

This other thing—this confusing, frightening sensation that tightened and melted her loins at the same time, this wild, sweet hunger that robbed her of the ability to reason—that she could cope with, too, given time. She'd been taken off guard, that was all. It had been so long since she'd experienced it. For years she'd unconsciously sublimated her desires into a driving energy that had seemed to burn even more fiercely when she'd entered her thirties. "Rune, look, I'm sorry if I—well, if I led you to believe I was willing to . . . you know. The thing is, I was married for literally half my life, and I can't shed that so quickly. In small towns like Morristown, where everybody knows everybody, the wives don't . . ."

"And the men do," Rune said dryly.

Miserably, Corey nodded. "Mine did." She laughed shortly. "It doesn't add up, does it? We're not really stuck back in the last century, but things just move a lot slower back home."

Leaning against the pillar once more, Rune crossed his legs at the ankles. "I wouldn't waste time worrying about it, honey. A lot goes on in any town that some people never know about. And you're—"

"Don't say it." Corey shuddered delicately. "I'm one of those depressingly nice women your mother keeps throwing your way. Want to know something funny?"

"Yeah, tell me something funny."

The gruff tone brought her eyes around. Corey hesitated briefly and then, with a small shake of her head that threatened the security of her topknot, she decided that honesty was the only possible policy between them at this point. "That list of mine? One of the things on it is: have an affair."

Rune's lopsided grin was perfectly visible in the light from the rising moon. "I believe I did mention a mutual aid pact?"

"I think if it's all the same to you, I'll just substitute something a little safer. An affair, when it's in the abstract, is one thing; when it comes down to actual practice, I don't think I'm ready yet."

Corey suspected she'd never really be ready. After a few months, having put her life into proper perspective, she'd go back to Missouri and settle down in a nice apartment with nice neighbors, and she'd find herself a nice job. Then she'd start shopping for a rocking chair and let the good times roll.

4

Rune toyed with the discarded husk of a sunflower seed as he stared at the intimidating sheet of paper in his electronic typewriter. In the upper lefthand corner was the legend, 73 Macklin/Animus. Halfway down, nicely centered, was the caption, Chapter Four. At this moment, he couldn't have said what chapters one, two, and three were about if his life depended on it.

"Damned interfering female," he muttered. He gulped the last of his gin and tonic and typed a name. *Corey.* What the hell kind of a woman was she, anyhow? Why had she chosen to disrupt his summer sabbatical?

"Cheap, sweet wine, iceberg lettuce, and well-done steaks." He shook his head, wondering how a man who'd always prided himself on having civilized tastes in all things could get hooked so quickly on someone like

Corey Peters. "A stereotypically provincial female if I ever met one," he condemned. If he had to have an unattached woman next door, why couldn't she have been the type who'd have enjoyed a simple physical affair?

From a nearby three-by-five-foot cage came a burst of Portuguese. "Stow it, Toad," Rune ordered without looking up. He'd long since given up on teaching the bird to speak English; at this point, he'd settle for a little less irreverence. The wise guy down in Brazil who had bonded this particular specimen evidently had one hell of a sense of humor.

Hunching his shoulders, Rune bore into his story, willing his subconscious mind to pick up the ball and run with it. He'd got as far as the delivery room scene, where the vital statistics of the Animus were being recorded as it escaped from the placenta and scurried up the wall.

Shortly after one he gave up. Three pages of drivel. Yesterday it had been four and a half. Damn it, he'd been going great guns for three weeks, and now, all of a sudden, he was drying up. And there was no real reason for it. The story was as sound, as tightly constructed, as it had been when he'd first conceived it, only he was sick to death of the whole tedious concept of a separate physical embodiment of the animal part of man's nature.

In the kitchen, he scowled at the gleaming white insides of the refrigerator and then slammed it shut to check out the sparse contents of the freezer. Where were all those eager females who'd practically force-fed him for the past few years? It had got to the point where he was almost ready to surrender to the inevitable and take on a wife just to protect himself from all that rampant domesticity.

Morosely, he stared through the screened window at the fenced-in pool, where Corey was spreading her towel and kicking off her sandals. Face it—in spite of all her denials, he'd been waiting for her to drop by with her own special bouillabaisse, or maybe a slab of the Grand Marnier soufflé she just happened to have whipped up.

"Your favorite foods? What a *coincidence!*" she'd coo breathlessly. "I was wondering what on earth I'd do with the leftovers, and I just happened to think of you—I do hate to see good food go to waste, don't you?"

Rune uttered a four-letter word he hadn't used since his undergraduate days. So all right, maybe he was doing her an injustice; maybe she'd never even heard of that damned magazine, but it was just too pat. The fact that the two of them just happened to be spending the summer in these relatively isolated cottages, sharing a swimming pool, sharing a beach. She was the right age, and far more important, she had an offbeat sense of humor that could become addictive if he didn't watch it.

What was it he'd been quoted as saying in that blasted article? That he liked his women with a sense of humor as well as a sense of adventure? That should teach him to keep his mouth shut; when he'd used those words to his mother, he'd been trying to explain why he couldn't abide a particularly dull woman she'd tried to push off on him.

She'd got even with him by giving an earful to that damned feature writer from *Southern Latitudes,* complete with the picture a local sports photographer had taken after one of last season's polo matches. The writer had tried to reach him a dozen times. She'd never made it past his sharp-eyed secretary. When he'd read the article a few months ago, he'd felt like slapping a lawsuit on everyone from the publisher down to the copy boy. It would have meant still more publicity, though, and by that time, the damage had been done.

Since then, in addition to fending off the daughters of his mother's friends from the Raleigh area, he'd had to start fielding women he'd never even heard of before. Like that call he'd got from the woman in Alabama two days before he'd left Raleigh. Before he could shut her up, she'd told him in embarrassingly intimate detail what she could do for him besides cook his favorite dishes.

And now here was this shrewd little number from Missouri who just *happened* to be staying all alone next door. And who just *happened* to have a sparkle of wit in those big gray eyes of hers, who dreamed up fantastic landscapes peopled with strange shell-creatures— although the article hadn't mentioned his interest in science fantasy—and who just *happened* to be extremely good-looking.

God, was she good-looking!

Restlessly, Rune prowled the rooms of his small cottage, returning again and again to the one that faced the swimming-pool enclosure. Both cottages were on stilts, which, unfortunately, gave him a perfect view into the pool enclosure. It might be just the thing for parents to supervise the kids at play, but damn it, he hadn't had a decent afternoon's sleep since he'd spotted her that first day, and his work was suffering for it.

It had been purely accidental, that first glimpse. She'd been wearing a relatively modest one-piece suit, and he wouldn't even have noticed the low-cut neckline or the high-cut legs except for the expanses of tender pink flesh they revealed. Any previous sunning she'd done had obviously been done in something even more conservative than the one-piece.

Rune had been gazing absently out the window, mulling over the relationship of a minor character to his hero. He hadn't been able to write anything worth saving the night before, and he knew he'd sleep better if he could bat out one decent paragraph first—even a sentence. After a while, the minor character had been forgotten.

The next day, the one-piece had been replaced by a string bikini, and he'd made no pretense of even trying to sleep. His schedule was shot to hell, anyhow. He'd started out writing nights because for years, that was the only time he'd had to scribble anything. Mornings he spent on the phone with the office, and once a week, he'd called his mother to assure her that yes, he was still alive, and no, he was not ready to reveal his whereabouts. Afternoons, when it was too hot to do much else, had been spent sleeping under the ceiling fan—until *she'd* come, and things had started to go haywire.

"Oh, hell," he growled.

"Corvo louco," the large green parrot responded.

"Polly want his throat slit?" Rune gave up. He couldn't sleep, he couldn't write, and unless he wanted to subsist on parrot-mix, grapes, and Chambertin Clos de Beze, he couldn't eat. At least, not until he'd made a run on the nearest supermarket.

And damn it, he couldn't even watch his neighbor with a clear conscience now that he'd met her officially and shared a meal with her. It wasn't the sort of thing a decent man did to someone he knew.

Toad protested his prolonged captivity by calling him a

crazy crow again, and sighing, Rune released the catch on the front of the cage. "All right, you old reprobate, climb aboard." He held his arm in position and waited while the parrot tested its security, first with his leathery tongue, and then by closing his knife-sharp beak gently on the proffered arm. The testing done, Toad stepped aboard, fluffed his feathers, and canted his head mockingly. A guttural purr of satisfaction emerged from his scrawny throat.

Corey was almost asleep when she felt something strike her back. Lazily, she swatted at it. A moment later, it came again. Retrieving the tiny shell that had caught her on the shoulder, she clutched her bra to her and rolled over onto her stomach, squinting against the sun.

"Hi," Rune called out from just over the fence. "Are you decent?"

"Of course I'm decent." Corey fumbled frantically with straps and ties. In desperation, she lunged for her turquoise cover-up and rammed her arms into the sleeves. "Isn't this your nap time?"

He stepped into the opening, to be silhouetted against a high brassy sun. "I couldn't sleep—thought I might talk you into going swimming with me."

"In the ocean?" Corey said doubtfully.

"You're at the beach, remember? You can swim in a pool back in Missouri."

"What about all the riptides and undertows and other ocean things?"

"Have you taken a good look out there in the past few days?" Rune dropped his towel onto a bleached cypress chair and sat down, tanned legs sprawled out before him. "Calm as a bathtub. There's not enough current to move a cork, believe me."

Corey drew her knees up and embraced them. "Hmmm. Still waters run deep," she murmured obliquely. "Were you throwing shells at me, or was it raining pennies from heaven?"

"I thought you might be asleep and I didn't want to startle you, but I promised my mother I wouldn't swim alone."

"You've got a real hang-up about your mother, haven't you?" Corey tilted her head and studied the lean, shaggy man in the chair above her. He didn't look like the apron-string type, but you never could tell. "Which are you looking for today, a baby-sitter or a lifeguard?"

"Take your pick," Rune offered magnanimously. He'd never before noticed what fascinating colors sunlight lent to black hair. Each strand glowed with an iridescent life of its own.

"I'm out of practice as a baby-sitter, and I'm afraid I never qualified as a lifeguard. You could always walk down to the motel beach; that's what I plan to do when I tackle the Atlantic."

"No need of that. You're in luck, because I just happen to be a bona fide certified lifeguard—at least I was a hundred years ago when I was young." Reaching for her hand, he tugged her to her feet, and Corey swayed before him, dizzy from the heat and possibly a lack of protein. She'd skimped on lunch, since she'd used up today's salad and cheese last night.

"Then, what in the dickens do you need me for?" she asked. "I'd probably fall apart if you got into any real trouble."

Rune held the gate open and then kept his arm at her back. Grinning down at her, he said, "Somehow, I doubt that. You strike me as the sort of woman who could handle most any emergency that came along."

"Just don't put me to the test. I wouldn't like to spoil all your illusions. Is it always this calm?" They stood on the top of the dune until her feet began to burn, and then, clutching his arm, she slipped on her sandals.

"Believe me, it can get rough. I've been coming down here since I was a kid, and I've seen the Atlantic join the Bogue during a hurricane. My folks used to have a cottage at Salter Path, just a few miles up from here. It was undercut by a storm back in the fifties, and since then, the property's all but disappeared. That's one of the problems with waterfront property; it has a tendency to melt."

"I wonder if Abbie knows?"

"Your cousin strikes me as a level headed woman. Besides, with the width of the beach along this stretch, I don't think she needs to worry."

"Have you known her long?" asked Corey, feeling a strange sensation that could almost be jealousy, although whether for her favorite cousin or her new friend, she couldn't have said.

"Didn't know her at all before I called last month. A friend told me about the cottage. He rented it last year. Lucky for me, it was still available, so after swearing him to secrecy, I rented the place for the summer."

Corey glanced up in time to see the look of annoyance flicker across his face. "Why the secrecy? Another little game with your mother?"

"Look, let's get something straight, shall we?" Rune said grimly, tossing his towel on the beach. "Contrary to what you obviously believe, I'm not all tangled up in apron strings. It just so happens that I admire my mother one hell of a lot. I wouldn't hurt her feelings for the world, but sometimes she bugs the hell out of me. Like on the matter of women. All her friends drag out these pictures of grandchildren for a tooth-by-tooth comparison, and she has to suffer through it in silence. I'm her one and only shot at posterity, and I've let her down, but damn it—"

Corey shrugged out of her shirt. "You don't have to explain anything to me, Rune. Believe me, I understand your feelings all too well."

"I doubt it," he muttered sourly.

The last thing she wanted to discuss was grandchildren—especially her own. She could do without being automatically bracketed in his mother's generation. Staring out over the placid aquamarine water, she murmured, "You're sure it's safe? No currents that are going to carry me off to Hawaii or Egypt or wherever?"

"Not too big on geography, are you?" Shaking off his momentary irritation, Rune grabbed her hand and led her into the cool white froth that laced the shallows. "I can't believe you've never been in the ocean before. What did you do for vacations?"

"Oh, sometimes we'd go to visit my grandparents in Topeka, and sometimes we'd go to a summer camp the church owned at Beaver Lake in Arkansas. Then, after I got married, we didn't go anywhere much. Couldn't afford it." As a small wave slapped cold water against her heated body, Corey gasped. "Rune, let's go back! It's freezing!"

"Take my hand," he ordered. "See that small wave coming? We're going to dive through it. I promise you, you'll love it."

Corey had time to utter one weak protest, and then it was either dive or be dragged under. She knifed through the clear water as cleanly as Rune did, and by the time she emerged again, she was laughing, still clinging to the strong hand that had guided her through and eased her back onto her feet again.

"What did I promise you?" Sunlight danced in the curls on his well-shaped head, on the lush piratical-looking mustache. Either she was getting used to him, or he was doing some discreet barbering. His eyes sparkled through a thicket of drenched lashes, and Corey thought he was quite possibly the most beautiful creature she'd ever beheld. As the seas eddied around her shoulders, she uncrossed the arms she'd crossed against the expected chill.

"It isn't cold at all," she marveled.

"Turn around, honey," Rune ordered gently.

Puzzled, Corey made one complete turn and came back to face him. He took her shoulders and turned her so that she faced out to sea with her back toward him, and then she felt his fingers at the tie of her bra.

"Oh, no!" To her horror, she found that she'd floated out of her top. Eluding his fumbling fingers, she sank beneath the surface and, holding her breath, struggled to recapture the ties she'd evidently failed to secure. One of the ends had tangled in her hair as she reached behind her, and she was quickly running out of breath.

Rune lifted her out of the water. Turning her in his arms, he held her against his chest. "You little idiot, what are you trying to do, drown yourself?"

"Why didn't you tell me?" Corey panted, still fumbling with the spaghetti strings, the long strands of wet hair, and the other pair of hands that were interfering with her progress. Pressed as she was against Rune's hard, warm body, her modesty was preserved, but her dignity was completely shattered.

"Hold your hair up out of my way, will you? Hereafter, you'd better stick to wearing that black and blue thing."

"What do you know about my black and blue thing?" Obediently, Corey gathered her hair up and allowed Rune to tie the bra strings.

"I saw it hanging on the line," he improvised quickly. He hadn't practiced law all these years without learning to think on his feet.

"Why didn't you remind me to change into something swimmable?" She tilted her head back to stare up at his angular jawline.

Rune shrugged. "Some of these things are pretty seaworthy. How was I to know you hadn't tied it in the back?" He finished the job, gave her a gratuitous squeeze, and stepped back, mustache twitching suspiciously.

Corey scowled. At the sound of his laughter, she scowled more fiercely. "What are you laughing at?"

"You. Standing there with your arms crossed over your chest like you were holding a litter of newborn puppies."

"You could have said something," she grumbled.

"Well, as a matter of fact, I was all set to ask for the one with the pink nose, but I thought you might get upset."

Corey stared in disbelief for a moment, and then she howled. A wave lifted her off her feet and she floated over it and resettled on her toes, still laughing. "You're perfectly awful, do you know that? It's a good thing for you that I happen to have a weakness for terrible old jokes . . . even when they're on me."

"It's a good thing for you that I happen to have a

weakness for women who enjoy terrible old jokes, and I wasn't laughing *at* you, but *with* you."

Corey thought it best to drop the whole subject. He'd been laughing at her, all right, but somehow, his laughter didn't hurt. Probably because Rune McLaughlin meant nothing to her, she rationalized. Or possibly because she enjoyed his company too much to risk losing it over something so trivial.

"Let's float over a few swells and then go in and get something to eat," he suggested. "I haven't had lunch yet."

Somehow, they found themselves floating side by side, joined by a hand and a foot. "I thought you slept through the afternoons," Corey called over the soft rushing sound of the water.

"Sometimes I do—lately I don't. Don't worry, if there's any change that affects Toad and Jack's routine, I'll let you know in advance." A slight current threatened to separate them, and Rune hooked an arm through hers.

Under the cerulean dome of a cloudless sky, they floated in companionable silence, hip jostling against hip, thigh against thigh. It was an oddly asexual intimacy. As one troublesome thought after another tried and failed to take root in Corey's consciousness, she began to relax still more. In fact, it had been years since she'd felt so completely at peace. Maybe she'd been meant to come here, to this barrier island off the lower coast of North Carolina. She could watch her troubles drift out to sea, and then, in her own good time, gather the strength to start rebuilding her life.

Idly, she examined the idea as a curious sense of detachment infiltrated her mind and body. With Rune holding on to her, she felt oddly safe. It was like keeping one foot on home base. As long as any part of her body was touching him, she couldn't be tagged out.

Which was absurd. Even among the wilder ideas she'd been entertaining lately, that one was outstanding for its stupidity.

As a light breeze sprang up, a wave lapped over her face, and stupid or not, Corey resisted the urge to grab him with both hands. The man was a perfect stranger, she reminded herself sternly—a hack writer with no visible means of support and a brand of charm that could easily become addictive. She'd read about the sort of men who flaunted their beautiful young bodies around resorts and preyed on susceptible women.

And she was susceptible, all right. The only other thing she was was reasonably smart. As long as she let him know she was onto his game . . .

"You're a beach bum, aren't you?" she asked, just to let him know she wasn't taken in.

"Hmmm?" He sounded as if he'd been half-asleep.

"Well, no offense, but you don't seem to spend much time servicing swimming pools, and you did say you've never published, so . . ."

"Ah, I see. The work ethic rears its ugly head. Did it ever occur to you, my dear half-reconstructed Corey, that I could be simply waiting for a rich widow to support me while I write the Great American Novel?"

"I'd guessed as much." Somehow, now that he'd admitted it, she found herself wanting to defend him. "Of course, there's the odd fact that you're scared stiff of women."

"Because I was wary with you, you mean? But then, you're not a rich widow, are you, Corey? How do you know what I'm like when I'm on the trail of big game? Maybe I was afraid you'd latch on to me and scare off my intended victim."

"Ha! Fat chance." She turned her head to grin at him, licking the salt from her lips. "I'll make a deal with you, McLaughlin. Teach me what I need to know about ocean-swimming and how to light a fire in the wind, and I promise you, I'll clear out at the first sign of a rich widow."

"I'll introduce you to every briny skill at my command, and I'll teach you to cup your match like a bos'n in the North Atlantic. That's two for one, pal. What else do I get out of this deal? Just staying out of sight's not much of a trade-off." Here it comes, he thought with a surprisingly strong surge of disappointment. Bouillabaisse and Grand Marnier soufflé.

"Gee, I don't know." Corey thought about it, not all that enthusiastic about the idea of his getting involved with another woman, but unwilling to admit it, even to herself. *Especially* to herself.

"How about this," she broached finally. "If you get a lead on a possible victim," she stressed the word slightly, enjoying his pained expression, "you may use my car say, three times a week for your dates, and if you bring her home with you, I'll baby-sit Toad so he won't spoil your romantic atmosphere with those insulting cracks of his."

Rune considered the offer from all angles. She was good. If she were a phony, then she deserved an Oscar. He discarded several rejoinders and went for an oblique approach. "How do you know they're insults?"

"My great-grandfather spent most of his life in Brazil as

75

a missionary. My father learned Portuguese as a child, and occasionally, in a moment of stress, he'd let something slip."

"And of all the cottages on this beach, you had to move in next door to a narrow-minded Amazonian parrot who refuses to learn a second language. It defies the odds, doesn't it?" In fact it reeked mildly of collusion. Rune steered them toward the shore again. "Did you mean it about the car?"

"Of course I meant it," Corey said quickly before she could take back her hasty offer. She'd been brought up on the parables: fox and sour grapes as well as dog in the manger. If she didn't want Rune McLaughlin, there was no reason to begrudge another woman his company. "Did you mean it about letting me swim with you and teaching me to strike a match in the wind?"

"My word is my bond," he said solemnly.

As they neared the shallows the gentle waves began to tumble about them. Rune stood up and waited until Corey got her footing, and then he said, "You're really a pretty decent sort, you know that? The truck doesn't exactly present the sort of image I'm looking for." Of course, neither did the gunmetal XJ12 he'd left with a retired judge in Swansboro, he admitted silently. The owner of the truck was doing active time for his second DUI, and the guy's grandmother, the judge's cook, had been glad to pick up a few dollars by renting it out. His own car was too easily recognizable, and he'd thought it wise to keep a low profile. If his mother discovered his whereabouts, she was apt to descend on him with her latest candidate.

Ashore, Rune suggested a run down the beach until they dried off. They alternately ran and walked for perhaps a mile, and then turned back toward the cottages again.

"I can't get over how lovely all this is," Corey murmured, her eyes on the glassy surface of the clear blue water.

"Nor can I," Rune replied, and she knew without looking that his eyes were on her. There was a deeper note to his voice, a soft huskiness that hadn't been there a moment before.

Halting, she turned to face him, completely unconscious of the way her thin cotton cover-up clung to the damp curves of her body. "Look, Rune, there's a chance that we can make it through the summer on pretty good terms, but you might as well know—in fact, I thought I'd made it clear last night—I don't play games. I'm not interested," she said, mentally crossing her fingers. Then she blurted, "Besides, I don't know how. If you want to be friends, then that's fine with me. If you want something else, I'm sorry. I'm flattered and all that, but I just can't handle it."

Rune stared at her, wondering if she was playing a game of her own. Flattered! God save the queen, what did she have to be flattered about? No woman with as much to offer as Corey Peters should be flattered by the attentions of an unkempt out-of-work beach bum. And as far as she knew, that was what he was. He was all but certain now that she hadn't the slightest idea that he was one of *those* McLaughlins—thirteenth-generation American, tenth-generation money, Cabinet members under three presidents and Supreme Court judges under two. Not to mention a plethora of other illustrious forbears.

Eyes narrowing against the sun, he hazarded a question. "What if I say I don't want your friendship? You say you can't handle an affair, but frankly, I don't think men and women were meant to be platonic friends."

Corey hid her disappointment under a careless shrug. "Then we'll go back to being strangers. I'll do my swimming at the pool or the motel beach, and you can find yourself another baby-sitter."

His bushy eyebrows took on a doleful slope. "Does this mean I don't get to use your car for my dates?"

Her chin dropped, and then she snapped it shut and scooped up a handful of gravel. "You wretch! You conniving, self-seeking *wretch!*" Just as he spun away, she hurled the gravel at his feet, and Rune took off after her.

They fell in a laughing heap at the top of the dune, and when their eyes accidentally met and tangled, it was Corey whose gaze slid away. She eased herself from his arms and brushed the sand off her damp shirt. "Is this Friday? I lose all track of time down here."

"Good. That's what beach vacations are for."

"Not so good if the supermarket closes before I get there. I'm fresh out of everything."

Efficiently, they gathered towels and sandals and turned toward the cottage. "Want to rinse off in the pool?" Corey suggested, oddly reluctant to see the afternoon end.

"How about the hose. I'll let you go first and use up all the hot water, and I'll take the cold."

Clutching her wet towel and sandy scuffs to her chest, Corey curled her toes against the gritty concrete walk. "What have you got against swimming pools?" she teased.

"Can't stand the smell of chlorine."

"You're in the wrong line of work, then, aren't you?"

Rune grimaced. He was sorry now he'd ever embarked on this foolish subterfuge. It was damned tiresome. On the other hand . . . One minute he was convinced she was on the level, and then she'd say something to make him wonder. "Look, Corey, there's something—"

"No, don't. It's none of my business what you do with your life, Rune. One of these days, when you hit the best-seller lists, you can thumb your nose at those of us who've plugged away all our lives at dull jobs and never got anywhere."

Mumbling something that sounded vaguely profane, Rune turned on the hose and tested the temperature. Then he played it over her feet and legs, rinsing off the sand. "Somehow, I can't see you wasting your life on anything humdrum, Corey. You never did say what you did. Teacher? Preacher? Indian chief?"

"What's the euphemism? Between jobs? I guess that about describes my position." As the water turned cold, Corey shivered and hopped aside. "Your turn. Sure you wouldn't rather brave the chlorine? It's warmer."

"What sort of jobs are you between? Maybe I could—"

"You're incredible, you know that? Don't tell me there are some openings in your line of beach-bumming."

Resigned, at least for the time being, to the role in which he'd cast himself, Rune stood his ground while she rinsed off the worst of the sand. "Do you type?" he asked, hopping around when the water turned icy.

"Nope."

"Keep books?"

"Nope." Household accounts hardly counted.

"Uh . . . retail experience?"

79

"Only as a consumer. Actually, I'm looking for an executive position. I'm good at organizing things and overseeing thousands of small details. I delegate well, but I'm not afraid to jump in and get my hands soiled in an emergency." Ha! And since an average day in the life of a homemaker produced approximately nine-point-seven emergencies, her hands usually stayed pretty soiled.

"You mentioned going to the grocers, Madam President. If I have my secretary make up a list and give it to your secretary, would you soil your hands to the extent of doing my shopping for me?"

"Only if you autograph it."

"Autograph it?" Puzzled, he took the hose and began to coil it up.

"The grocery list. That way, I won't have to stand in line for your autograph when you're rich and famous. See? I told you I was good at organizing. Efficiency, that's my middle name."

Uncoiling the hose swiftly, Rune aimed a shaft of cold ground water at her stomach, and Corey screamed.

5

~∙∞∞∞∞∞∞∞∞∞∞~

The champagne was waiting for her when she got back to the cottage. Arms laden with sacks of groceries, Corey managed to pull open the screened door and let herself onto the porch, but she was juggling too many things at once. The keys fell to the floor, and she swore impatiently. It was late and she was starving. The crowds at the checkout line had been long, but she'd entertained herself with thoughts of sharing another meal with Rune.

Naturally he'd invite her, as she'd done his shopping as well as her own. There was really no reason why she shouldn't accept. His order had been mostly for frozen foods, the expensive, already-prepared kind, unfortunately. She hadn't quite dared to substitute cheaper items. Maybe later, when they got to know each other better, she could give him a few friendly hints on shopping more wisely.

Bending at the knees, she eased one heavy bag down into Abbie's chair and turned to place the other one on the table, and it was then that she saw it, a bucket of half-melted ice that held a bottle of—with one hand, Corey angled the bottle so that the label showed. Champagne?

"Well, bless his sweet little heart," she murmured, feeling a constriction in the region of her chest. "He didn't have to go that far."

Still, she thought with a rising feeling of excitement, it boded well for the rest of the evening. There was no harm in drinking to a budding friendship, was there? Something a little less festive might have been more appropriate, but who was she to quibble? Writers—novelists, she corrected—future best-sellers, she tacked on generously—probably went in for grand gestures as a matter of course. Back in Morristown, Missouri, a six-pack of diet cola would have served the purpose.

She put her milk and meat in the refrigerator and decided the rest could wait until later. Glancing in the mirror, she brushed a hand over her hair, smoothing the flyaway strands and tucking them neatly under her topknot. And then she deliberately plucked them out again, fluffed them up, and studied the effect before going back to the car for Rune's groceries.

The truck was missing: that was the first thing she noticed. The second was the note he'd stuck in his screen door, asking her to please put his frozen food in the freezer, that he'd probably be late getting home.

"Well, *darn!*" Corey said plaintively. Shrugging, she let herself into the kitchen. He'd left the back door unlocked, and the light on the top of the range for her to see by.

At a low scratching sound from the next room, she

lifted her head in the task of adding the stack of expensive prepared frozen dinners to the few remaining in his compact freezer. "Rune?" she called hopefully. "Rune? It's me, Corey."

Toad. She identified the covered cage, and the small illogical hope died. Struggling against an unreasonable feeling of disappointment, Corey let herself out.

Idiot. Imbecile. Stalking back across the gritty pavement that circled the pool, Corey chided herself for all her foolish expectations. It had been obvious from the first that he wasn't there. The truck had been missing, and as if that weren't enough, there was the note. Had he asked her to dinner? Of course he hadn't. Had he even mentioned seeing her later? Not a word.

But there was the iced champagne, she countered wistfully. Before she could rein it in, her intractable imagination was busily at work, visualizing Rune in lean black pants and a flowing open-fronted silk shirt. He'd got as far as her porch when he'd heard his phone ringing. Expecting an important call from his publisher, he'd left the wine and dashed back. Only instead of a publisher—Corey skimmed over the small fact that so far, he didn't even *have* a publisher—it had been a beautiful, rich twenty-four-year-old widow who just happened to be looking for a talented virile young novelist to sponsor. Rune, of course, had raced to her side, all thoughts of Corey and the champagne and the frozen dinners forgotten.

Sighing, she let herself into her own porch, collected the dripping bottle, and took it in to the refrigerator. She shoved it to the very back, behind the milk, the orange juice, and the kosher dills, and then she tipped the melting ice into the sink.

A simple thank-you would have sufficed, she thought irritably. Next time he could do his own darn shopping.

The following morning when she left the house for her walk, Corey saw that her grill had been freshly scoured and relined with foil. She glanced at the moisture-glazed screens of the cottage next door, wondering if Rune had already left for his walk. Perhaps he'd be waiting for her on the dune when she got back. She'd have to thank him. Champagne *and* a scoured grill was really going too far. He was one favor ahead of her, and now she'd have to think of some way to even the score.

Either he'd walked earlier, or he'd decided to wait until later. Corey hung around the beach, ostensibly collecting shells, until clouds obscured the sun. And then, carefully averting her face from the other cottage, she trudged back to her own.

Rain. The weatherman had promised it as a relief from the sultry heat, and from the looks of the sky, he was a man of his word. Which meant no beach-walking, no swimming, and no sunning. And no Rune, she added morosely.

As the clouds thickened out over a milky-green sea, she wrote a long letter to Winnie, extolling the many pleasures of a beach vacation and asking about nursery colors. Then she wrote to Abbie, addressing the letter to a hotel in Zurich. As the afternoon wore on and the rain set in, she paced, always returning to stare out the south window at the square gray shape across the pool.

The pickup truck was back in its customary place beside the mulberry tree, gleaming wetly and looking, for once, almost respectable. Where the devil had he gone last night? At least a dozen times during the day Corey had reached for the phone, only to turn away again. A simple phone call to express appreciation; certainly no one could find fault with that, she rationalized, but still . . .

By the middle of the afternoon, she finally worked up her nerve to call. She actually had the phone in her hand when it occurred to her that she didn't know his number. She wasn't even sure the cottage had a phone, and if it did, how would it be listed?

In frustration, she uncovered Abbie's portable sewing machine. It had been years since she'd sewn. At one time in her life, when Winnie had been small and she'd been housebound, she'd taken pleasure in making clothes for them both. It had been necessary if she wanted anything decent to wear. Ed had often bragged that no wife of his would ever work, and in the beginning, she'd been too naive to see the irony of that statement. Fortunately, she'd always had plenty of energy, as well as a sense of humor. It had taken both to get her through the lean years of keeping house, raising a child, and helping out at the store.

From the looks of her sewing cabinet, Abbie had stocked enough material to last a lifetime. Corey fingered a length of yellow and white striped muslin. If worse came to worse, she could always run up a pair of nursery curtains, or another beach cover-up—or maybe a tote bag out of that scrap of red burlap.

By late afternoon, the rain was still falling heavily. In desperation, Corey rolled up the legs of her coveralls and pulled on Abbie's yellow plastic raincoat, determined to walk the beach until she was tired enough to drop. The sou'wester style hat refused to fit over her hair, and swearing, she took down her knot and began stuffing the thick coil haphazardly under the voluminous brim. As fast as she got one side under cover, the other side slithered down about her shoulders.

"That does it," she muttered impatiently, reaching for the phone book and turning to Abbie's handwritten list on the back page. "Hair—Milly." Trust Abbie to reduce everything to the basics. Bank, Cottage, Dentist, Doctor, Drugs, Hair, Garbage . . .

Cottage. "Of course!"

But first the hair, Corey decided. Now that she'd finally made up her mind, she'd hate for the place to be closed. She was in luck. Milly could cut her hair at eight-thirty on Monday morning if she didn't mind coming in that early. Corey didn't. "The sooner the better, before I start to have second thoughts," she said. "See you Monday."

While her reckless mood lasted, she dialed again and listened until the buzzing sound on the other end was abruptly broken of. "Rune? It's me, Corey. I just wanted to say thank you."

At the lengthening silence, her stomach began to tighten. Had he been writing? Or sleeping? Surely he hadn't been serious about the rich widow. Oh, horrors, maybe he'd brought her home with him last night, and they'd been . . .

"I guess I caught you at an awkward time," she said diffidently.

"No, that's all right. I was writing, as a matter of fact. Corey, would you mind telling me how you got this number?"

"It's in Abbie's phone book under Cottage. That's the way she lists things—sort of generically, you might say."

"Okay, just curious. And by the way, thanks for—"

"Please, you don't have to thank me. *I* called to thank *you*."

"Look, this could get maudlin. Do you mind if we just skip it? I've finally got the old muse working again, and I don't want to let her escape, so if that's all . . . ?"

A moment later Rune sat holding the phone, cursing himself for an insensitive, unfeeling bastard. She'd pinched off a little apology for disturbing him and hung up before he could retract. Reaching for the instrument again, he punched out the first few digits impatiently, and then he slammed down the receiver. Use your head, McLaughlin!

He sprawled in his chair, scowling at the scattering of seeds and tiny green feathers that littered the floor. He'd lay odds she was over there squirming with embarrassment, and he'd just made it worse. And damn it, that was the *last* thing he wanted to do. How the devil could a woman reach her age and still be so damned naive? She'd probably never in her life given a man iced champagne before, or wine of any sort. She'd be the sort who considered such a gesture strictly a man's prerogative. Like initiating a phone call. And he'd cut her off, and now he could kick himself.

He'd just have to find some way to make up for it without getting himself involved any deeper. After cleaning her grill in exchange for her doing his shopping, he'd planned to ease off. The plain truth was, she was beginning to scare the devil out of him.

A wintry smile flickered in his eyes as Rune thought of their unprepossessing beginning. He'd known a lot of women, most of whom had passed in and out of his life without leaving a trace. There'd been one, back when he'd been about twenty-four. . . . It hadn't worked out, but he'd worn the scars for a long time.

The trouble was, he couldn't pin a label on Corey Peters, and it irritated him. She stubbornly refused to be filed away and forgotten. Somehow, he found himself wasting whole hours on adolescent daydreams. He was thirty-nine, damn it, not fourteen!

"If my mother could see me now, she'd move in for the kill," he muttered in grim amusement to the parrot who continued to regard him with cynical orange eyes.

Shifting his gaze to the bottle he'd found on his porch this morning, he shook his head. Resting in a plastic bucket of tepid water, it was probably not the worst champagne available, but it certainly wasn't one he'd ever subjected his palate to. Fortunately, she hadn't been around to witness his reaction when he'd found it. The rather obvious ploy had surprised him. The lack of taste in wines didn't. Still, he wouldn't have hurt her for the world.

And damn it, that was the thing that had him baffled, that he *cared*. That he actually cared more for her feelings than he did his own gut. Hadn't he eaten her thin overdone steak and her bland salad? Next thing he knew, he'd be drinking her cheap wine, unsavory additives and all.

Why the devil had he lied to her about his writing? He hand't written a line worth keeping in days. All he could think about was the way she looked reaching around to smooth oil over the backs of her thighs, the contrast of her long tanned hands against her round white breasts when she'd stroked the oil on her vulnerable upper regions. Her hands had moved slowly at first, and then much more quickly as if she felt some obscure guilt at finding pleasure in the touch of her own flesh.

Even her laughter got to him, damn it. The sound of it—the way it started as a dancing light behind those somber gray eyes of hers and then suddenly burst forth like the Fourth of July.

"Oh, for crying out loud!" Rising abruptly, Rune raked a hand through his hair and began prowling the confining space of the living room.

"Ladrão, ladrão!" squawked Toad, as he paced back and forth in his cage.

"Yeah, for once you're dead right, old fellow. She's a thief."

Someone had stolen his powers of concentration in the last few days, not to mention his peace of mind. And the only new element in his life was Corey Peters. Last night, in an effort to gain a little perspective, he'd gone to visit Judge Burrus in Swansboro. They'd played chess until Mrs. Burrus had finally run him off, and it hadn't helped at all. He'd crept in like a thief in the dark, afraid of turning on a light, afraid she'd call out from her porch to say good night, and he'd go over there and . . .

Corey machine-hemmed the yellow and white striped cotton on all four sides and then wondered why she'd bothered. Maybe she'd embroider daisies on the edges. Did anyone actually need a thirty-six-by-forty-seven-inch tea towel these days?

The weekend had ended with no sign of Rune. Short of smoke billowing out of his roof, nothing would make her seek him out again. Her ego was on the mend, but she wasn't about to subject it to another rejection.

On Monday morning she awoke with a sense of renewed purpose. This was the day she got on with her project, the reconstruction of Corey Peters. She'd clipped a picture from one of Abbie's magazines showing a hairstyle that was conservative, but still casual. It was short, but not too short, fashionable without being extreme. Now, if she could just locate the place before she chickened out.

Her car wouldn't start. She ground the starter until the battery threatened to die, and then she strung together every swear word she knew. And then she got out and kicked the tires and swore again. Finally, she slammed into the house, marched to the phone and canceled her appointment.

The sun was already heating up the air, and her temper tantrum hadn't helped. And all that hair was a burden she simply didn't need. Grabbing the scissors from the sewing basket, she stood in front of the mirror and took a deep breath. For years she'd cut Winnie's hair. There was no reason why she couldn't cut her own. Milly could trim it up for her later; all she wanted to do now was to get it off her neck.

Closing her eyes, Corey started whacking. The scissors slipped harmlessly over the bulk of the swath, but at least she'd started something. There'd be no backing out now. Grimly, she watched the drift of ebony strands collect around her feet as she cut first one side and then another. By the time both sides swung freely above her shoulders, her anger had dissipated and stark terror was beginning to set in.

"Corey?"

She jumped, and the scissors took a scalloped bite out

of the left side. Oh, Lord, the last thing she needed now was an audience.

"Corey, are you in there?"

She heard the screen door slam, and then he was looming in the kitchen doorway, shutting off the light, demanding to know just what the devil she thought she was doing.

"Look what you made me do!" she accused, pointing the gleaming blades at the uneven left side.

"What *I* made you do! Have you gone crazy? First I hear you out there swearing and kicking tires, and now you're in here *ruining* yourself. What's got into you?"

Reaching behind her, Corey gathered up the untouched length still to be cut. From just behind her, Rune's image glowered at her in the mirror. "I decided to cut my hair," she informed him, the glint of challenge in her eyes.

He snorted expressively. "Another stage of your reconstruction?"

"Why do you insist on making me sound like an urban renewal project? If I want to change my hairstyle, is that any business of yours?" What had started out as a declaration of independence somehow ended on a defensive note as she added, "Besides, it was hot."

"Well, it's a damned fool thing to do when you've got hair like that, not that you asked my opinion."

"No, I didn't."

"You could at least have had it done professionally. Frankly, it looks like hell right now."

Scissors aloft, Corey stared pointedly at Rune's unkempt head of shaggy curls, and the mustache that gave him such a piratical look when he was angry. Someone had been trimming on them since she'd first seen him. They were considerably neater, but they were still a long way from Morristown standards. "As it happens, I had an appointment with Abbie's hairdresser, but my car wouldn't start, so I had to cancel. The next opening wasn't until Wednesday, and by then I'd have lost my nerve."

"I saw you kicking the tire. Didn't it help?"

"You didn't see me driving off, did you?" she snapped back, wielding the scissors in irritation.

Rune took them from her hand before she could do any more damage. "At least let me even up the back for you. If I've got to look at you for the next few weeks, I don't want you looking like a vagrant sheepdog."

"What's the matter, have you got a patent on that style? No, in your case, I think Irish water spaniel would be more appropriate. All those salty, shaggy, sunburned curls."

Snatching the remaining hank of long hair, Rune led her forcibly out to the porch. "My curls are neither shaggy nor salty. Now pipe down and be still before I end up scalping you."

"Ouch! That pulls." If she'd had a hand mirror, she wouldn't have let him within a country mile of her head. As it was, she could use some help, and he was all there was. "Not too short," she cautioned. "I want to take it in easy stages until I get used to it."

He was standing behind her. She couldn't see what was going on, but she could feel the heat of his jeans-clad body, the brush of his arms on her shoulders, his fingers on her nape. She could feel his intense concentration as he gathered up small sections of hair and cut through them. The scissors made a dry sound, and drifts of hair feathered down her back. Squirming itchily, it occurred to her that she should have changed into an old shirt. Except that she didn't own an old shirt anymore.

"Isn't that about short enough?" she murmured timidly after several minutes of silence.

"Do you want it even or don't you? You took a big chunk out of the left side, you know. I can either trim it all to that length or scallop the right side and the back to match."

"Don't you dare!" She had a vision of an inverted picket fence hanging just below her ears. Oh, Lord, why had she ever started this mess?

"You might want to let a professional give it a touch-up when you have time. I don't know much about ladies' styles."

"Maybe your rich widow will teach you." Corey regretted the words as soon as they were out. They reeked of fox and sour grapes.

"My rich widow?" He sounded almost as if he'd forgotten, and then he said, "Oh, I have no doubt that my rich widow will teach me any number of things."

Corey blew a dusting of hair from her cheek and then ventured to ask the question that had pestered her all weekend long. "So you've found one. That was quick work."

The scissors went still, and then Rune laid them on the table. "Yeah," he murmured after a barely perceptible pause. "Things were just beginning to get interesting when she sent me home. I'll have to admit, though, that it was a smart move. That's where an experienced woman has the advantage, don't you think so? They really know how to use mental foreplay to the best advantage."

Corey's mouth fell open, and she blinked several

times. Mental foreplay? Great Scott, she'd never even heard the term, much less thought about it.

From beside her, Rune reached out and closed her mouth with a gentle thumb beneath her chin. "You're really going to have to stop doing that, honey. The mosquitoes will be thicker than ever after all this rain, and I'd hate to see you inhale one."

"Rune, you shouldn't talk that way," Corey said reprovingly. She stood up and began to brush the hair from her skirt with agitated movements.

"Why not? It's true—people do it all the time. I knew a fellow who inhaled a bee once. Now you talk about trouble, he had it. We rushed him—"

"That's *not* what I meant and you know it!"

"It isn't? What did you mean?"

"*You* know. What you said. It certainly isn't the sort of thing a man discusses with a woman he hardly knows."

"You mean mental foreplay? What's the matter, honey, do women in Morristown consider foreplay a dirty word?"

"Would you *stop it?*" She could feel the heat rise painfully to her face, and she groaned. In a woman of her age, blushing was absurd.

"Don't you know that a woman's most erogenous zone is her mind? I learned that before I was twenty."

"I'll just bet you did." Seething, Corey made intricate work of raking her shorn hair into a pile. How on earth had they ever got off on such a topic, and why, for goodness' sake, couldn't she learn when to shut up and let well enough alone? "Look, thanks for the haircut," she said grudgingly as she edged toward the kitchen door. "Now, if you'll excuse me . . ."

"You're not going to wash that stuff down the drain, are you?"

"What stuff?"

"The stuff you've got in your hands. The stuff that's stuck to your dress and your arms and your neck. Don't you know what hair does to septic tanks? Don't they have septic tanks in Missouri?"

Grimacing at the cloudy dark mass, she said, "Well, certainly they have septic tanks. I mean, they must—I mean, I've never had one personally, but—"

"Big problem." Rune nodded sagaciously. "Usually clogs up the trap before it ever gets as far as the tank. Sand and hair—it's what makes the plumbers so successful around these parts."

Biting her bottom lip, Corey glanced at the trash basket in the corner of the porch. "Abbie didn't mention it."

"She didn't know you were going to chop off your crowning glory."

Dumping the hair, she brushed off her hands and then started in on her dress. "Crowning glory, my foot. I'd have done it years ago if I weren't such an awful coward. I guess I should thank you, Rune. I'd probably have botched it if you hadn't stepped in."

Rune's face softened in a slow smile. "Go change into your bathing suit and we'll get you cleaned up before you start itching. Hang your dress on the line so the wind can dust it off. In case we ever get another breeze."

Corey's own breathlessness had little to do with the suffocating stillness of the weather. How could things look so calm on the surface and yet feel so stormy?

His eyes followed her as she disappeared into the house, and then he loped across to his own place. It had come to this, he thought with bitter amusement: the senior partner of McLaughlin, McLaughlin, Disher, and Pinke had stooped to lying, cheating, and conniving, and all for a woman he'd known barely a week. Heaven help him when she got a look at herself in the mirror.

The ocean was no longer the pellucid blue it had been before the rain. In her black and blue maillot, Corey stood on the beach ten minutes later and considered the possible effect of hair on the swimming pool filter as she waited for Rune to join her. Experimentally, she shook her head and winnowed her fingers through her remaining hair. She felt light-headed, in more than one sense.

"Did you look in the mirror?" Rune called out as he topped the dune.

"I didn't have the nerve. It feels wonderful, and if it looks awful, I'd just as soon not know it." Clasping her hands over the sides of her head, she waited for him to join her. Not even her concern over her freshly butchered hair could keep her from appreciating his lean, fit body.

He was so different from the muscle-bound superjocks Ed had always admired. The breadth of Rune's shoulders and the narrowness of his hips was more a matter of bone structure, the lean, hard musculature only enhancing the flawless foundation. He'd look marvelous in a three-piece suit. She wondered idly if he'd ever owned one.

"You'll do," he dismissed, joining her at the edge of the surf. "Come on, what are you waiting for?"

"I told you I was a coward. It looks much colder today. Maybe I'll just stick to the pool."

"Oh, no you don't, my shaggy little mouse. I'm responsible to Abigail for that filter. Come on, we'll dive

ENTER THE
Silhouette Diamond Sweepstakes

WIN The Silhouette Diamond Collection

Treasure the romance of diamonds.
Imagine yourself the proud owner of
$50,000 worth of exquisite diamond jewelry.

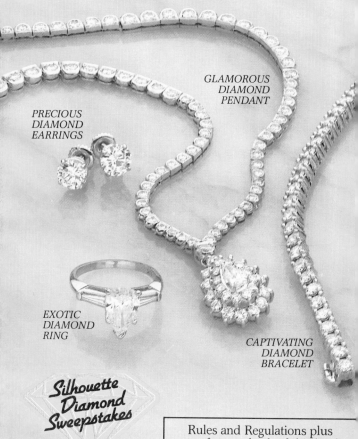

GLAMOROUS
DIAMOND
PENDANT

PRECIOUS
DIAMOND
EARRINGS

EXOTIC
DIAMOND
RING

CAPTIVATING
DIAMOND
BRACELET

*Silhouette
Diamond
Sweepstakes*

Rules and Regulations plus
entry form at back of this book.

in together. After the first wetting, you'll be warm as toast."

"Could I have that in writing?" she stalled, laughing reluctantly as he dragged her nearer and nearer the frothing surf.

"Warm as toast—you have my personal guarantee."

6

By the time Corey had been subjected to half an hour of Rune at his most charming, her suspicions had grown too strong to contain.

"What the devil did you do to me, anyway?" she demanded breathlessly, hair on end and a streak of gravel dripping from the side of her face. She'd taken all the contact sports her puny powers of resistance could handle, and the minute she'd pulled away from Rune's solicitous arms, she'd been tumbled end over end by a nasty little wave.

"Are you accusing me of ducking you?" Rune asked in hurt surprise.

Corey clutched handsful of ragged hair and yelled, "My hair, you idiot, my hair! Is this why you keep staring at me like that? Have you done something awful to my head?"

Rune did his noble best to keep a straight face. "Honey, I only did what I could to salvage the chewed up mess you'd already achieved. I never claimed to be an expert at ladies' barbering."

With a small groan, Corey covered her face with her hands. "You've ruined me for life." Another wave struck her on the back, and she staggered. "That does it. I've had enough. With all this sand churning around, this is worse than the Mississippi, and you know what they say about that."

"Can't say that I do," he drawled, withstanding the surging seas with maddening ease.

"That it's too thick to swim in and too thin to plow," Corey snapped.

Suddenly he was standing within arm's reach again, water glistening on his mustache as it twitched in an engaging grin. "But it's just what I ordered. It takes a surf with a little power behind it for what I'm about to teach you."

"Maybe you could teach me in the pool."

"Bodysurfing?" Rune crowed disbelievingly. "Honey, even back in Morristown folks must have some idea what it takes for surfing . . . unless you Missourians have some pretty terrific Jacuzzis."

"Yes, well, I suppose it does take waves, but I may as well warn you, Rune, I'm not the athletic type."

"Oh, come on now, you swim like a fish. Everybody has some athletic ability."

"Not me. I learned to swim because the church camp had a swimming instructor who threatened me with a five-mile hike through poison-ivy country, and I stayed in practice because I happened to be the only mother free to cart all the kids on our block to the pool and stay with them."

"So you'll probably never make the Olympic swimming team; there are other sports. Surfing's mostly a matter of coordination. How's your tennis? Your golf?"

"My tennis? I'll put it this way, the pro uses me as an example of what not to do. I took golfing lessons to please Ed. I was lousy." Her mind had usually been on things like whether or not the Children's Home van had had its brakes relined on schedule, or whether anyone had checked to see if old Mr. Henderson had ever located his glasses. The least of her worries had been whether a knotty little ball fell into a hole in the ground.

"Scratch golf and tennis," Rune murmured with a shrug. Come to think of it, it had been years since he'd made time for a game of either. "How about skiing?"

"Sorry."

"Checkers?" he asked a little desperately.

"Now *that's* my sport. My daughter, Winnie, and I used to play a lot. I was teaching her chess when—"

"You play chess?"

"Not awfully well, I'm afraid. I only managed to beat my father twice, and one of those times he was recovering from flu."

A wave, larger than the rest, cracked her on the shoulders, and Corey staggered into Rune's arms. With razor-sharp reflexes, he took advantage of the situation to press her sleek, if nonathletic, body against him and bury his face in her hair. She smelled of an enticing mixture of wildflowers and saltwater . . . and looked, he admitted with half-fearful amusement, like a molting porcupine.

"It is a little rougher today. Must be a storm offshore," he murmured, his lips moving against her forehead. His tongue emerged surreptitiously to catch a drop of salt-water before it could drip down into her eye.

Rune could picture a small replica of Corey, eyes grave and mouth determined as she concentrated on learning the various values and moves of the game of chess. He dismissed the possibility that she could resemble her father in any way. She was Corey's daughter. Although Peters, he grudgingly admitted, must have had something on the ball for her to have married him in the first place. Rune, somewhat to his surprise, found that he resented the unknown man as he'd seldom resented a rival before.

A *rival?* What the devil was he thinking about? Corey Peters was strictly a temporary part of his life. Once this brief respite was ended, he'd go back to the suite of offices that had once been occupied by his father and resume his share of the work load he'd shifted onto the shoulders of his partners, Merrill Pinke and Abe Disher. In time, he'd pick up where he'd left off with the three or four women whose company he enjoyed, and do his best to avoid the rest. By then the effects of that damned article would have faded.

And Corey? Standing hip-deep in the cool, sudsy waters of the Atlantic, Rune knew a moment of acute dismay. Who'd be holding her come autumn? Another poor fool like the first one she'd married, a clod who lacked the sensitivity to see beyond the seductive body, the surface prettiness?

Or would she wait for someone who could appreciate the real loveliness that lurked beneath all that? Someone discerning enough to appreciate the way her eyes could go from anger to gravity to laughter in the space of a single minute, the way her mouth could quiver on the edge of laughter and still manage to look incredibly passionate? And that streak of outspoken honesty that came through at unexpected moments . . .

Speaking of honesty, Rune reminded himself as his arms tightened imperceptibly, maybe it was time for a little honesty on both their parts. But then, he hadn't actually *denied* the fact that he was a member of a respectable profession with an excellent income independent of the two large trusts he'd inherited.

He hadn't actually *denied* the fact that he was a lying, conniving bastard whose sole aim was to get this woman into his bed, either, Rune reminded himself with brutal honesty.

Corey, knowing she was shamelessly taking advantage of the situation, savored the feel of his rugged strength, the masculine scent of his body. She was like a kid given a big bag of candy—even knowing she'd pay for it later, she was determined to enjoy as much as she could cram in now.

"Rune? You mentioned teaching me something about bodysurfing?" she reminded him hesitantly when her conscience prodded her into action. She could stand here hanging on to him all day, but it would make it just that much harder in the end. She'd always known the value of self-honesty; Rune was a pleasure she could enjoy in small doses, and for a limited time only. He was definitely *not* a taste she could afford to cultivate.

"Hmmm, I do seem to remember mentioning it. On the other hand, we could always practice being a lighthouse. That way we get to stand here indefinitely and warn unwary mariners off the dangerous reefs."

The dangers Corey was wary of had nothing to do with

reefs. Reluctantly, she disengaged herself from his arms. Taking a deep, slightly unsteady breath, she turned stoically to confront the incoming tide. "Well? Shall we saddle up?"

For the next forty-five minutes, Rune patiently instructed her in the simple art of judging, timing, and then launching herself for the exhilarating shoreward ride. Time after time Corey floundered impotently back at the starting place as she watched him streak all the way in to shore.

Finally, winded and limp from exertion, she clung to his hand as they waded ashore after the last semisuccessful ride. "I warned you," she panted. "I'm just not the athletic type."

"Sleep on what you've absorbed this morning. Tomorrow it will come as natural as breathing," Rune reassured her, squeezing her hand and resisting the desire to sweep her up in his arms and bury his face in those heaving breasts.

"Thanks for the vote of confidence," Corey gasped. "In case you hadn't noticed, I can't even manage breathing at the moment."

"Oh, I'd noticed, all right," Rune replied softly, his eyes never leaving the quivering cleavage exposed by her low-cut suit. "At least we managed to wash all the hair off your chest."

Laughing in spite of herself, Corey jerked her hand free and turned away. "Just keep your impertinent eyes off my chest, if you don't mind."

Rune's arms closed around her from behind, and he drew her against his own chest. "There's no hair on your back, either, in case you were worried about it," he murmured into her ear. "And as far as I can see, your lovely little back porch has been swept clean, too." His hand curved over her hips, one finger daringly raiding the high perimeter of her suit to emerge with a cargo of gravel.

Corey found it impossible to be angry with him. She found it impossible even to think of anything except the arms that were clamped around her middle, the tautly muscled body braced so tightly against her back. They were separated by no more than a few thin layers of wet fabric, scarcely enough to disguise the effect her nearness was having on him.

It was reciprocal. As his taut hardness thrust against her soft buttocks, she found herself unconsciously pressing against him. She swallowed hard. "Rune . . ." she began uncertainly, but she didn't want to protest. What she really wanted to do was so shockingly explicit in her mind that a small groan escaped her parted lips.

Sun beat down from a cloudless sky, and Rune closed his eyes, the better to bring into play his other senses. Lord, she felt marvelous. She'd feel even better without all this wet stuff between them. Sleek and slender and soft in all the right places, she had a woman's body, and he was achingly aware of the fact that it was wonderfully designed to complement his maleness.

His hands slipped up to cradle the soft underswell of her breasts through the clinging cloth, and then eased upward until he felt the rigid nubs of her nipples. Had he had this effect on her, or was it just the cold water?

A light aircraft buzzed intrusively overhead, reminding him of their lack of privacy, and he swore silently. His timing left a lot to be desired. If only they were already inside, showered and relaxed, with the bed a few feet away. As it was, it was going to require some careful maneuvering on his part to get her back to the cottage without breaking the mood.

Visualizing her nude body, sleek and golden tan except for a pale, intriguingly shadowed little triangle, Rune searched his mind for a tempting lure. "Corey, can you visualize a tall, cool gin and tonic somewhere out of this blazing sun?" he whispered seductively. "We wouldn't want you to get blistered, would we?"

Standing rigidly in his arms, Corey was afraid to trust her powers of visualization another inch. They'd already proved to be shockingly creative. Struggling to wrench her mind away from the growing demands of her body—obviously, Rune had managed to accomplish it with no trouble—she tried for a light, carefree touch. "I must be tuned to a different channel: that's not exactly the picture I'm getting."

"It isn't?" he replied, eagerness showing through the ragged holes in his composure.

Ignoring the sudden tightening of his arms, Corey said, "Picture this: On a wicker table next to a tall, frosted glass of iced tea with a juicy wedge of lime glistening on the delicate rim is a thick, luscious sandwich of lusty, spicy corned beef, crisp, succulent young cucumbers, rich, creamy mayonnaise . . ."

Dropping his arms, Rune stepped back and gritted his teeth. He didn't know whether to laugh or cry. Was she being deliberately provocative, or . . .

Oh, hell, it was probably too soon, anyway. Divorcée or not, she just wasn't the sort of woman a man could rush. Next time, though, he'd set the scene more carefully. Like hooking the screen door, taking the phone off the hook, and hanging out a yellow fever flag to repel all boarders.

"Yeah, now that you mention it, that doesn't sound half-bad. I vote for kosher dill pickles, videlia onions, and a hot, salty mustard instead of cucumbers and mayo."

They topped the dune and paused. In the humid haze of the midday heat, Corey's dress hung limply on the clothesline.

At least we've got the yellow fever flag flying, Rune thought wryly. It's a start, at least.

"The mulberries are all gone," Corey observed as they trooped up the steps, and then she giggled. "Rune, do you have any idea how funny you looked the first time I saw you, in nothing but your drawers, all red-faced and streaked with mulberry juice and cat scratches?"

"If you ever dare mention that to a living soul, I'll sue you for—"

"For what, telling the truth? The eccentric novelist— maybe it'll give your career a boost."

Rune had caught the legal term just before it had left his tongue. Damn it all, he couldn't even tease her without tripping over his own deceit. Thoroughly disgusted for letting himself get embroiled in such a juvenile farce, especially at his age, and with his experience, he wondered how the devil he was going to get out without convincing her in the process that he was a certifiable jackass.

Oh, sure, it might have been a reasonable precaution at first, but why had he let it go on this long?

The cool, analytical portion of his brain rattled out an answer that didn't please him at all. The fact that he hadn't come clean after the first few days was an unconscious admission that he needed all the protection he could get from Corey Peters. The next logical question was *why?*

"Iced tea?" Corey asked, going to the refrigerator and removing a platter of corned beef, along with several jars. A little guiltily, she hid the bottle of champagne he'd given her behind a quart of orange juice. She should have at least sampled it by now, but she'd preferred to forget the whole embarrassing episode.

"How about trying a gin and tonic?"

"How about milk?" she parried.

"Done." Slicing off a sliver of the beef she'd cooked the day before, he lifted his eyes in surprised appreciation. "Hey, this stuff's great!" He cut himself another slice while Corey began spreading whole wheat bread with Abbie's Pommery mustard. If he could compromise on the matter of drinks, she could try mustard instead of mayonnaise.

"Want some of my cucumber?" The cottage felt comfortably cool after the broiling heat of the midday sun. At least she hoped it was that that had produced the goose bumps on her thigh when she'd accidentally brushed against him. They'd both jerked back, and from then on, she'd been careful not to get too close to him.

"I'll give up my pickles in favor of your cucumber if you'll put a slab of onion on both our sandwiches." Locating the glassware, he poured two large glasses of milk.

"It's a deal," Corey pronounced. She failed to add that she always had onion on her corned beef sandwiches.

Rune leaned back against the counter, feet braced apart, arms crossed over his chest, and a totally untrustworthy grin on his face. "Good. Because I intend to build up my strength with one or two sandwiches first, and then I intend to kiss the living daylights out of you. And I'd really hate to have to go home to brush my teeth and gargle first. You see, I'd planned this sort of spontaneous approach, and something like that reeks of forethought, don't you think?"

After the first startled instant, Corey collapsed in laughter. The heated skin of her back touched the cool steel of the refrigerator door, and she gasped and jumped away, still laughing. "So much for spontaneity. What do you think you are, a dessert?"

"Actually, I'm much better as a main course if you'll give me half a chance to prove it," Rune returned with a leer.

"Thanks, but I prefer corned beef to ham."

"And I prefer tongue to cheek," he shot back.

Brows lifting despairingly, Corey groaned. "Slow up, will you? We country girls aren't as swift with the repartee as you clever city boys."

"Raleigh hardly ranks as a metropolis," Rune said wryly. Nor was it by any means the sum total of his experience, he neglected to add. Considering a diversionary tactic appropriate, he nodded to the remains of the corned beef. "Was that thing already cooked, or did you have to do something besides thaw it?"

"That's my mother's recipe. It's always a hit at the Fourth of July picnic and the volunteer fire department's fund-raising suppers."

"So how come you never learned to cook a decent steak?"

"What's wrong with my steak?" she demanded, instantly on the defensive.

Rune carried the plate of sandwiches out to the porch

while Corey collected the napkins. "Other than being criminally undersized, not to mention carbonized, not much," he said carelessly.

"For your information, I like my beef well-done."

"For your digestion, you should learn the difference between leather and beef. That so-called steak you served the other night could have resoled a pair of boots, if there'd been enough of it."

Plopping herself down across the table from him, Corey snatched one of the thick sandwiches from the plate and glared at it. "You had the largest portion, and I noticed you didn't leave much."

"I was starving." Rune bit into his own sandwich and moaned his appreciation. "Now this," he said when he'd swallowed, "is about as close to perfection as a corned beef sandwich gets. Pumpernickel or rye might have been—"

"If you don't like it, you know what you can do with it!"

"Didn't I just tell you it was perfect? Honey, perfection comes in a variety of flavors, believe it or not." He took another generous bite and leaned back in the wicker chair.

"Not when it comes to beef, though, right? It has to be just the way you like it or it's imperfect. You're just like my ex-husband."

Struggling to sit up, Rune attempted a protest. Unfortunately, with a mouth full of corned beef, there wasn't a whole lot he could say at the moment.

"Ed always knew best. *Always*. About *everything*! There was a time when I liked my steaks thick and slightly pink, but no, Ed had to have them bloody and quivering like a bowl of cherry jelly inside."

"Couldn't you simply leave yours on the grill a few minutes longer?"

"You don't know Ed," Corey said grimly. "By the time the fire was ready, the beer had been flowing long enough so that nobody could argue with him. It wasn't worth trying. I learned to feed my steak to the dog and linger over the rest of the meal, and he was usually too busy being the genial host to notice."

How on earth had she wound up with an insensitive clod like that in the first place? He knew the type, and he avoided them whenever possible. "You entertained a lot?"

"Oh, Ed was big on entertaining," she said bitterly. "The more the merrier."

Something in her tone led him to believe that the company hadn't been any more to her liking than had the menu. He was beginning to understand a few things about Corey Peters. He found he wanted to know much more. "Tell me about your little girl, Corey. Is she staying with the grandparents, or does her daddy have her for the summer?"

Frowning, Corey took a large bite and chewed slowly. When she'd finally swallowed it, she gulped down her milk and then reached for her sandwich again, and Rune watched her, amusement at her transparent tactics giving way to thoughtfulness. Trouble over visiting rights, unless he missed his guess. And something about the situation still bothered her. He knew from experience that some mothers found it damned hard to let go of their offspring.

Uncomfortable over her own evasiveness, Corey jumped up from the table and began sweeping up her crumbs. "I'd better get this cleaned up," she muttered. "Ants, you know."

Oh, Lord, he obviously thought Winnie was still a child. She hadn't realized she'd been quite so successful in her role as a carefree young divorcée. What would he say if he learned that not only was she the mother of a grown, married daughter, but that in just a few months, if all went well, she'd be a grandmother? The very term implied a gray-haired respectability that was the antithesis of the image she'd been trying to promote.

Oh, blast, Corey wailed inwardly, why couldn't she have got away with it for just a little while longer? She hurried into the kitchen and began rinsing milky glasses as if her life depended on it, and Rune followed her. She could sense his puzzlement, but for the life of her, she didn't know how to deal with it without telling him the whole thing. She'd never been good at dissembling: her mind didn't work that way. She'd have been better off going with Abbie and her tour group of retirees. At least she'd have had nothing to hide.

A mystery woman. She scoured furiously at the flower-patterned countertop. That usually implied a woman with a hidden past, not a woman with a hidden future. Did the glamorous connotation still apply?

The fist clutching the wet sponge slowed, and gradually a dreamy expression darkened her eyes. Years from now, when she was baby-sitting, perhaps teaching her granddaughter to bake coconut fingers or to play checkers, it would be nice to think that somewhere in the world there was a heartbreakingly handsome man who remembered her as an attractive, mysterious woman who'd dropped into his life for one brief, enchanting moment, and then disappeared without a trace.

7

~oooooooooo~

The days were smothered under a stifling layer of humidity. Air conditioners droned and dripped, and electric fans made a lethargic effort to move the heavy air. Nights brought little relief.

Corey and Rune met each morning at the top of the dune, sometimes hardly speaking at all. There'd been a certain amount of constraint between them since that day he'd taught her to bodysurf, and Corey blamed herself for that. He'd left soon after lunch, and Corey had tried to read, then tried to sleep, and finally ended up walking for miles on the beach and then going to a movie.

Now, as a sullen red sun dragged itself up from the watery horizon, they walked and talked. A tacit moratorium seemed to have been achieved as far as their relationship was concerned; they explored the more distant reaches of each other's minds, observing the boundaries of personal privacy, and Corey found her opinion of Rune as a person deepening and broadening to a faintly alarming degree. He was an immensely complex man, warm, witty, extremely well-informed, and far less the iconoclast than she'd first thought. If she wasn't careful, Corey knew with dismaying certainty, she could find herself falling in love with this man.

They put together haphazard lunches, usually cold cuts and iced drinks, and argued amiably over preferences in food and music, favorite comic strips and favorite editorialists. Having a man treat her as an individual with opinions worth hearing was a novelty in itself, and Corey reveled in it.

By the end of the week they'd covered national politics, agreeing in most cases, noisily disagreeing in a few. The subject of polyandry came up, and after walking for miles and then cooling off in the tepid ocean, they dropped down onto the sand to explore it, disdaining the use of towels.

"Polyandry's no good," Rune dismissed. He was on his back, head resting on his crossed arms. "One woman, several husbands? It'd never work today. Women far outnumber men, so it just doesn't make sense. Polygamy, now, that's another thing. Let the women share the few remaining men among them."

"Some of us already have," Corey observed dryly, and then could have kicked herself for injecting the personal into a purely objective discussion. Lately she'd begun to take pride in her ability to handle a platonic friendship with a stunningly attractive man. For the most part, she was able to ignore the feelings he aroused in her, the dreams that left her limp and longing and vaguely unsatisfied.

Rune rolled over onto his side and propped his head in a sandy hand. "The ex-husband? Ah, honey, I'm sorry."

"No, I'm the one who's sorry, Rune. I don't know why I even said that." Her voice, curiously muffled, was almost lost in the lazy shuffling of gravel in the nearby surf.

"We all speak from a personal bias, Corey, no matter how objective we try to be. Now, you take me. . . ."

"Not even with green stamps," she retorted, grateful for the lighter note. Was he even aware of the subtle tension that seemed to shimmer in the air when they were together? Was it all in her imagination? He'd wanted her once—there were some things a woman couldn't be mistaken about. Perhaps he'd reconsidered the wisdom of getting involved in a summer fling.

Or perhaps he'd seen through her disguise as a glamorous, carefree young woman to the very ordinary creature she really was.

"As I was saying," Rune stressed with wounded dignity, "you take me; my personal perspective is that of the hunted minority. In other words, I have to watch my step if I don't want to wind up gracing the harem of some predatory female."

"I thought that was the ambition of all you practicing gigolos." Corey turned to face him. Unthinkingly, she reached out to brush away a greenhead that had been tormenting them both, and Rune captured her hand and tugged her off balance so that she fell against him.

"My ambition, friend and neighbor, is to be the hunter instead of the hunted." Playfully, he dribbled sand above the low-cut maillot.

"And you only hunt big game," Corey affirmed. She

was having trouble with her breathing again, and it wasn't just a matter of humidity.

"The biggest," Rune growled. He buried his face in her thick, salt-damp hair. She'd had it trimmed by a professional, but not before he'd admitted to himself reluctantly that even with the hacked-up job he'd done on her, she was incredibly appealing. There was something about this woman. . . .

"Well, don't practice your marksmanship on me," Corey said a little desperately. "I'm strictly small game." The scent of him, clean, salty, masculine, was corroding her powers of resistance at an alarming rate.

"Don't ever mistake quantity for quality," Rune murmured a moment before he turned her face up to meet his.

After the first electrifying contact, Corey was awash with the knowledge that her whole week had been leading up to this. Her whole life could have been but a prelude to this single moment.

The kiss, enticingly seasoned with sand and sea, was brought swiftly to the boiling point, and then allowed to simmer slowly as its flavor and sweetness grew more and more concentrated. Rune rolled onto his back and drew her on top of him, tacitly allowing her to assume control. His hands arranged her for maximum contact and then began a slow, sensuous exploration. She was a delectable weight, her softness pressing him into the sand as he fought to restrain his swiftly rising passion.

Not so fast, McLaughlin, Rune cautioned himself, wondering what had happened to that cool, analytical brain that had always served him so well in the past. Unfortunately, Corey Peters had a way of making so much vanilla pudding of his much-vaunted mental faculties, including his usually dependable power of resistance.

Corey was having trouble with her own powers of resistance. The physical side of her life had been sublimated for so long, and now, after years of wading about in the shallows, it was as if she'd been suddenly thrown into a deep, raging tempest.

"This is crazy, you know that?" she gasped, lifting her head for air. What she lacked in experience, she was more than making up for in enthusiasm, exploring the taste and texture of him, savoring the coffee and toothpaste flavor of his mouth, the impressively responsive body beneath her.

"Absolutely non compos mentis," Rune groaned softly, "but don't let that slow you down." Somehow he'd managed to ease the straps of her suit down over her shoulders so that her naked breasts were pressed against his sandy, hairy chest. His hands moved agitatedly from the sides of her breasts to the gentle swells of her buttocks. As the thrusting tension of his loins increased dangerously, he pressed her hips tightly against him, seeking relief, finding only further incitement. Air whistled rawly through his clenched teeth. "As I see it," he grated, "we have three choices."

Corey, her trembling hands stroking the sides of his lean, muscular thighs, must have made some sort of reply. With the thunder of their heartbeats echoing the pulsating surf, she felt as though she were clinging to the slopes of an active volcano.

"We can try to make it back to the cottage." Rune punctuated the gruff words with small moist kisses that covered her eyes, her temples, followed the slope of her cheekbones. "Or we can risk getting hauled off to jail for public lewdness."

Breathlessly, Corey laughed. "Is that what we're doing? Or being? Are we against the law?"

Easing her slightly off to one side, Rune drew up his knees and grimaced. "It travels under a lot of euphemisms, honey, but when you try it in broad daylight on a public beach, you're apt to find yourself the star attraction of the next court docket."

Corey's hands slipped under the loose legs of his swimming trunks to make a daring foray onto the satiny skin of his hips. "Hmmm, lewd. It has a ring to it, doesn't it? Maybe I should have put that on my list: Learn to be more lewd and less ladylike."

Suddenly, she found herself on her back, gazing up at dangerously narrowed eyes, eyes that were so dark as to be impenetrable. With exquisite restraint, Rune allowed the very tip of his tongue to trace the curved line between her lips until, helpless with need, she took him in.

Clinging tightly, legs entwined in a vain attempt to ease the intolerable craving, they devoured each other. Corey had never wanted any man so much as she did this one. He was a driving hunger, a desperate thirst, a need that trampled out all reason.

She twisted her head aside. In an effort to hang on to a shred of reality, she whispered, "You mentioned a third option."

"I did?" Rune's voice was like ragged velvet. "Oh, yeah, we could always take a long, cold, exhausting swim."

"Are you offering me a choice?" She could hardly think; she certainly wasn't up to making decisions.

Rune began brushing the sand from her breasts with

his mustache. When his tongue sought the tightly furled nugget, a plaintive broken note issued from her lips. "Rune, I can't concentrate when you do that."

"They're like delicate little coral flowers." Rune kissed first one rigid bud, then the other. "Small, fragile, shy." He suckled gently, sending shafts of agonizing pleasure to the very roots of her body. "Look, see how they shrink away when I touch them?" He laughed softly, gazing down at her sandy breast as if it were a fascinating new discovery.

"What's your choice, sweet Corey?" he asked, lifting his eyes to meet hers. "Shall we take our chances with the law?"

Suddenly, it was as though the very air had been sucked from her lungs. She couldn't breathe. There was an odd whooshing sound overhead, and she clutched Rune's shoulders as the whole world became a blur of brownish gray.

"What the—*Corey, get down!*"

There was no time for gentleness. Rune pressed her painfully into the sand, covering her body with his. His arms bit into her sides, and she could feel his sandy legs scrape harshly against hers as his toes dug fiercely into the sand, grappling for security. "Jesus," she thought she heard him say prayerfully.

Aeons later—probably less than a minute—he was on his knees beside her, half-lifting, half-dragging her up into his arms again. Clinging together, they watched in awe as the roaring maw of a sand-clogged waterspout lifted branches, a section of fence, what might have been the cover of a utility trailer, and moved out over the sound, scattering its random possessions in its wake.

The silence of the aftermath was a tangible thing.

Stunned, Corey stared at the naked stretch of beach that led directly between the two cottages. She was dimly aware of Rune's voice, but the words seemed to have no meaning, no relation to the horrendous force that had just passed over them, leaving them miraculously untouched. She'd seen a tornado once from a distance. The ocean-going version was every bit as devastating.

"Are you all right? Corey, for God's sake, say something!"

Blinking, she shook herself back to a semblance of normality and said the first thing that popped into her mind. "Who *was* that masked man?"

"You little—!" Rune shook her, hard, and then he stood and helped her to her feet. "Come on, clown, let's go see what's left standing. I didn't see any roofs sail off over the sound, but I don't mind telling you, my eyes were shut tight there for a few seconds."

"You're going to have a nose-shaped bruise on your chest."

"Never mind the bruises, honey, do you have any idea how lucky we were?"

"Or unlucky, depending on the way you look at it. It was almost as if it saw us on the beach and . . ." Thoughtfully, she paused. "Rune, that wasn't another one of your options, was it?"

"My options?" They were walking awkwardly, holding each other in a mixture of fear and relief rather than passion. He grinned down at her. "Honey, I might make the earth move for you, but waterspouts are a little beyond my power."

"Do they happen very often?" She was rapidly revising any possible plan to resettle here on the coast.

"Not often. I've seen several offshore. Once when I

119

was a boy, I saw three at one time, but I've never seen one come in before. Still, it does happen. Every year or so you hear of one or two sweeping in and demolishing a narrow stretch of beach development."

"At least the cottages are all right." They paused at the top of the dune, surveying Abigail's property. "The fence . . ." A section of fence was missing from the pool, the rest of it untouched.

"There's a screen torn on my porch. Oh, Lord, I'd better check Toad," Rune muttered, starting down the dune at a trot.

"Jack was inside . . . I think. Oh, Rune, do you suppose—Rune, look! The pool!"

"Well, I'll be damned."

The pool was dry. One of the cypress chairs was overturned, one was precisely where it had been, cushion intact, and one was missing completely.

"The laundry! My yellow dress was on that line," Corey wailed, and then, "The mulberry tree!"

A survey of the damage revealed nothing more serious than a screen that had been torn when a table had gone through it, two windows totally devoid of glass, and a ton of sand in every conceivable nook and cranny of both cottages. The mulberry tree had been so severely pruned that its recovery was doubtful, and there was no sign of the clothesline or its contents. A highway sign had been deposited in the front seat of Rune's truck, via the windshield, and both that and Corey's car had been sandblasted.

"Toad's all right, but the poor devil's in shock," Rune reported back after they'd split up to check on the two animals. "He doesn't appear to have suffered any real damage, but he's already started plucking the feathers out of his breast. That's the equivalent of chewing his nails to the quick."

"Jack's asleep on my bed."

"It'll take more than a waterspout to intimidate that battle-scarred old veteran," Rune observed. He'd changed from trunks into jeans, and for the first time since she'd met him, he was wearing shoes. "Better get something on your feet, honey. Those two windows might still be around here somewhere, along with Lord knows what else."

"Power's off," Corey informed him. "I was going to make coffee."

"Phone's out, too, but I expect the line crews will be along pretty soon. Unless there were more of these things, the damage should be fairly localized."

"I don't know where to start," Corey said helplessly. She hadn't changed out of her bathing suit yet, and now, looking down at herself, she sighed. "I should have known I couldn't change my whole personality just by throwing out all those jeans and housewifely outfits and filling my closet with glamorous resort wear. Which do you think I should wear for excavating the kitchen, my white linen windowpane-checked culottes, or the salmon pink silk trousers with the tie-dyed overblouse?"

Stepping back, Rune eyed her hips consideringly. "I could lend you a pair of jeans. Let's take a closer measurement," he murmured, drawing her against him and then sliding his hands from his own hips to hers. "I think we could work something out here, don't you?"

His voice grew muffled as he buried his face in her throat, and with a desperate half-laugh, Corey pushed against his chest. "Remember what happened the *last* time we started fooling around. Don't tempt fate, Rune."

"Don't tempt *me*," he came back, sliding his hands inside the sleek fabric of her suit to cup the cool, smooth flesh of her buttocks.

Corey felt the rapidly rising tension in his lean, hard body as he pressed her to him, but she refused to fall under his spell so easily this time. She needed to think, and she couldn't, not when he kept setting off all these fireworks. "Stop it, Rune. You're—you're contagious. Look, do we shovel this stuff, bulldoze it, or vacuum it?" she asked, her voice stretched thin with her desperate attempt to ignore what was happening to them both.

Exhaling expressively, Rune put her away from him. "Do you know what's wrong with you depressingly nice women? Your priorities are all screwed up, that's what's wrong with you."

Covering her dismay—she wasn't aware that he'd bracketed her quite so firmly in that category—Corey turned to survey the discouraging mess around her. It was as if someone had thrown buckets full of sand through every window in the house. There was even a brier woven neatly into the living room screen.

"We'll shovel, then sweep, and then I'll see if I can round up a shop vac for your place. Toad's paranoid about vacuum cleaners since a fastidious friend of mine, a *former* friend, I might add, attempted to clean out his cage while he was still in it."

"Toad and the vacuum," Corey said dryly. "I wondered about that." Another of those depressingly nice women, if she remembered correctly. She'd have to try and dispel the image.

At Rune's suggestion, they worked on her place first to give the parrot time to regain his composure. Corey made a pitcher of iced tea and a plate of sandwiches, and then they declared the refrigerator off limits until the power came back on.

Shortly after dark, Corey begged a recess. "Rune, I'm bushed. I'm hot and tired and hungry, and if we work until midnight, we still won't finish. And then there's your place. Why don't we clean ourselves up and go out to eat?"

"Did it occur to you, honey, that with no electricity, there'll be no showers?"

Corey groaned. "And no swimming pool, either. How the devil did it swallow up all that water?"

"Slurp."

Laughing tiredly, Corey tossed a pillow at him. She'd been about to hang it on the line until she remembered that the clothesline was probably somewhere over on the mainland by now. "Then let's go swimming."

"Skinny-dipping?"

"In case you hadn't noticed, I'm still wearing a bathing suit. Why should I take it off to go swimming?"

"Honey, if you don't know . . ." Rune grinned wickedly.

"Rune, will you stop it? We have work to do!"

"Don't worry, I get the message." He laughed ruefully. "I'm probably too tired, anyway. Meet you at the beach in five, okay?"

8

Under a pale sliver of moon, a sea like liquid pearl reached out to infinity before them. "There's no current to speak of," Rune reassured her. "All the same, we won't go out too far."

"Maybe if we just sat down here in the shallows and swished around," Corey suggested, suddenly hesitant. The thought of being alone on a moonlit beach with a man like Rune was beginning to have a peculiar effect on her nervous system. Nor were all the dangers aquatic.

"Sorry, honey, I draw the line at swishing. And even at slack tide, there's enough wave action here to fill your suit with gravel. The whole idea of this exercise is to get ourselves cleaned up . . . isn't it?" He gave her a playful tug, and the gleam of his grin was not altogether reassuring. "Come on, my Missouri chicken, I'll hang on to you. Let's go wash the real estate off our respective hides." His hand sloped over her shoulder, slid down her arm, and captured her fingers. Wading out with her, he said, "We'll take that second one, shall we?"

As the slow, crestless wave approached, Corey clutched his hand and took three deep breaths to saturate her lungs with oxygen. At this point, hyperventilation was the least of her worries. "Don't let go of my hand," she cautioned, bracing herself for the long, shallow dive.

One strap had slid down when she broke the surface again. Laughing, she released Rune's hand to snatch it up, and then she raked the dripping bangs from her forehead. "You're a marvelous underwater swimmer. You could have gone much longer, couldn't you?"

"No more than another four or five minutes," Rune lied modestly.

"I'll bet! Where do you get your wind?"

"It's required in my profession."

"Really?" Corey tiptoed over a lazy wave, then she spread her arms and let her feet drift to the surface. The water was like cool, dark satin gliding over her body. "Calluses on certain portions of your anatomy I could understand, but I never knew good lungs were a requirement for a writer."

Rune grimaced. It had to come out sooner or later, he supposed, but he'd hoped for later. "Actually, I moonlight a bit." He launched himself onto his back beside her and captured her hand, tucking it into the crook of his arm and anchoring it against his body.

"Sure, but I didn't think you actually dove into the swimming pools and swam underwater to clean them out, or change the filters, or whatever it is you do. Isn't there an easier way?"

Ah—!" Rune bit back a rude word. "Honey, I'm a lawyer. As for the writing, it's strictly incidental."

After a long moment, Corey said quietly, "I don't understand."

He wasn't sure he could explain without getting in over his head. Weighing his words, Rune said, "I've always had an urge to try my hand at writing science fantasy, but there were all those years at school, summers spent law-clerking, and then, after I started practicing, the pace got even worse. Any time I could spare was devoted to something strenuous enough to work off the flab and frustrations. I sort of gave up on the writing. Oh, I'd get what I thought was a great idea now and then, but before I could follow through on it, it had gone cold." He risked a quick glance at her flawless profile. It was beaded with water, limned by a silver line of moonlight, and he wondered, not for the first time, how a summa cum laude graduate with a highly respected law practice could have managed to make such a jackass of himself in such a short time.

She hadn't moved a muscle. Floating there beside him, she could be asleep for all he knew. Clearing his throat rather self-consciously, Rune went on. "So when certain things began to pile up on me last month, I figured it was as good a time as any to get out from under and give it a shot. I'd been pushing pretty hard for the past several years."

Corey didn't know what to say. Oddly enough, she found that she wasn't terribly surprised. Hurt would be a more apt description for the feelings that kept her silent. Hurt and confused.

Rune respected her silence as long as he could, and then he said tentatively, "Corey?"

"Then you were just joking about cleaning the pool and the hair in the filter and swapping your labor for rent." Accusation was implicit in her tone.

"I never said I swapped my labor for rent," he said, and Corey didn't argue. Maybe she'd just assumed it. She'd assumed a lot of things, it seemed. "Look," he said earnestly, gesturing with his free hand. "I told Abigail I'd keep tabs on the commercial service that takes care of the pool. It's run by one of her ex-students—evidently she's got 'em all over the Southeast, and she said this kid had never been too reliable. All I did was promise to see that things get done on schedule. As for the filter and that business about the septic tanks, you might as well know the worst: when it comes to that sort of thing, I'm completely helpless."

Rune never thought he'd see the day when he'd find himself apologizing for being a lawyer instead of a plumber. "Corey . . . Honey, you're not mad at me, are you? It was never my intention to deceive you."

Liar! That plea wouldn't stand up in any court in the land.

Corey's laughter had an oddly strangled sound, even to her own ears. It must be the effect of water lapping around her head. This whole scene, she decided, was simply unreal. It was as if she'd suddenly become someone else, a woman who swam in the moonlight on pearlescent seas with dangerously attractive men instead of good old Mrs. Peters, who always ended up feeding, ferrying, and supplying dry towels for half the school-age population of Morristown, once the board of commissioners got together and pushed through the town's first public swimming pool.

About the only thing that Corey had in common with

this unfamiliar creature was gullibility. It seemed that neither of them had a grain of judgment where men were concerned; they'd believe anything they were told.

Abruptly, Rune let his feet drop to the bottom. His sudden move caught Corey unprepared, and she kicked out wildly for balance as the water closed over her face. Sputtering, she righted herself, only to be captured in the warm prison of his arms. "I'm sorry, I'm sorry, I'm sorry," he crooned.

"I don't want your stinking old apologies!" She pushed against his chest, only to grab onto his neck when a wave toppled her off balance.

"Corey, try to understand; I thought I had a good reason for not playing it straight with you. I didn't know who you were. How could I know you were going to mean so much to me?"

That was a low blow. He really must think she was dense if he thought she'd fall for a line like that. "You knew who I was, all right. I thought we'd agreed that I'm one of those depressingly nice women you despise so much," she flung at him bitterly. She struggled to escape the feel of him, wet-slick and blazing hot under a deceptively cool surface, but those smooth, rocklike muscles of his were incredibly strong.

"I finally came to my senses. I'm wild about depressingly nice women," he teased, catching her chin between thumb and forefinger and tilting her face to the moonlight. "Corey, please don't shut me out."

He was doing it to her all over again, and damn it, it wasn't fair. He had so many weapons; she had so few. "What if I told you I was a friend of your mother's?" So all she had was a slingshot; at least she knew where to aim.

You know the thrill of escaping to a world of PASSION...SENSUALITY ...DESIRE...SEDUCTION... and LOVE FULFILLED...

Escape again...with 4 FREE novels and

get more great Silhouette Desire novels —for a 15-day FREE examination— delivered to your door every month!

*S*ilhouette Desire offers you real-life drama and romance of successful women in charge of their lives and their careers, women who face the challenges of today's world to make their dreams come true. They are not for everyone, they're for women who want a sensual, provocative reading experience.

These are modern love stories that begin where other romances leave off. They take you *beyond* the others and into a world of love fulfilled and passions realized. You'll share precious, private moments and secret dreams...experience every whispered word of love, every ardent touch, every passionate heartbeat. And now you can enter the unforgettable world of Silhouette Desire romances each and every month.

FREE BOOKS

You can start today by taking advantage of this special offer— the 4 newest Silhouette Desire romances (a $9.00 Value) *absolutely FREE,* along with a Mystery Gift. Just fill out and mail the attached postage-paid order card.

AT-HOME PREVIEWS, FREE DELIVERY

After you receive your 4 free books and Mystery Gift, every month you'll have the chance to preview 6 more Silhouette Desire romances—*before they're available in stores!* When you decide to keep them, you'll pay just $11.70, (a $13.50 Value), *with no additional charges of any kind and no risk!* You can cancel your subscription at any time just by dropping us a note. In any case, the first 4 books and Mystery Gift are yours to keep.

EXTRA BONUS

When you take advantage of this offer, we'll also send you the Silhouette Books Newsletter free with every shipment. Every informative issue features news on upcoming titles, interviews with your favorite authors, and even their favorite recipes.

Get a Free Mystery Gift, too!

EVERY BOOK YOU RECEIVE WILL BE A BRAND-NEW FULL-LENGTH NOVEL!

Escape with 4 Silhouette Desire novels (a $9.00 Value) and get a Mystery Gift, too!

CLIP AND MAIL THIS POSTPAID CARD TODAY!

Silhouette Desire®

Silhouette Books, 120 Brighton Rd., P.O. Box 5084, Clifton, NJ 07015-9956

Yes, please send me FREE and without obligation, the 4 newest Silhouette Desire novels along with my Mystery Gift. Unless you hear from me after I receive my 4 FREE books, please send me 6 new Silhouette Desire novels for a free 15-day examination each month as soon as they are published. I understand that you will bill me a total of just **$11.70** (a **$13.50** Value), with no additional charges of any kind. There is no minimum number of books that I must buy, and I can cancel at any time. The first 4 books and Mystery Gift are mine to keep, even if I never take a single additional book.

NAME _____
(please print)

ADDRESS _____

CITY _____ STATE ____ ZIP ____

SIGNATURE (if under 18, parent or guardian must sign).

Terms and prices subject to change. Your enrollment is subject to acceptance by Silhouette Books.
SILHOUETTE DESIRE and colophon are registered trademarks.

CT 1835

His face in shadow, Rune examined her features as if he could see into her mind through the windows of her large gray eyes. Such clarity, he mused—grave one minute, laughing the next. And those dark, level eyebrows, the straight, honest little nose, and that chin that could be so determined without losing one whit of its femininity.

And the mouth. Oh, Lord, yes, the mouth! Groaning, he knew that no matter what she was, he had to have her. "Are you?" he demanded softly, gruffly, as the tide began to turn and a wave, larger than the rest, lifted them off their feet.

Mesmerized, Corey whispered, "Am I what?" Her legs tangled with his, and she fought desperately to regain her balance.

"A friend of my mother's?"

Her shoulder strap had fallen again. This time she ignored it. Caught in the dark web of his gaze, she defended herself as best she could.

"You'll just have to trust me, won't you? *Trust,* that's a five-letter word meaning—"

"God, Corey, don't do that to me." Rune ground out the words. Angry frustration drove him to conquer her mouth with bruising forcefulness. She was helpless to escape his crushing embrace, his scalding kiss, and all too soon her struggles ceased. Wave after wave swept around them. The tide had truly turned, but they were both caught up in an irresistible tide of their own making.

It was pitch dark and oppressively still when they finally mounted the dunes. They were lucky even to have made it to shore. Corey tried to convince herself that it had ended with that wild, dangerous kiss, but she knew better. It was a miracle that they'd managed to keep from drowning. Her suit was now hanging about her waist, her whole body quivering with the sensory memory of his touch.

"Power's still off," Rune observed, the words prosaic, the tone decidedly ragged.

"No fans." Corey tried to match his matter-of-fact approach.

"We can always sleep on the beach," he suggested, leading her down the back side of the dune toward her darkened cottage. "Watch it, don't walk into the pool."

"Mosquitoes," she murmured, but her mind was not on insects, nor empty swimming pools, either.

At the top of the steps, Rune held the screen door and allowed her to precede him. Tensely, Corey waited for him to bid her good night. Because if he didn't, if he followed her inside, they both knew exactly how it would end.

At the kitchen doorway, she halted, barely able to make out Rune's dark form against the dim glow of the sky. "Well," She laughed dismissively. "At least I won't stay awake all night reading."

"You've been having trouble sleeping?" His voice poured over her like warm honey. "Me, too. Must be something in the water."

"Rune," she began, and then his arms came around her again. The high, sweet singing in her blood effectively shut out the cool voice of reason.

"Corey," he groaned, burying his face in her wet mop of hair. "Ah, Corey, if you only knew how many times I've thought about this." His palms warmed her breasts, and when he captured her nipples between his fingers, a streak of molten silver shot through her body. It was all she could do not to sink to the floor.

She made one last colossal effort. "Rune, I told you, I'm not ready for this sort of thing." She'd all but forgotten that her suit was still hanging from her waist, and when she felt it being peeled over her hips, she clutched his arms. "Rune, please don't—"

"You mean you don't want us to make love? Can you honestly tell me that you want me to go home and leave you alone . . . *now?*" His voice was a soft rumble that registered on her body like the low notes of an organ.

She couldn't honestly tell him anything. Stepping out of the wad of damp nylon, she felt herself being swept up into his arms. It was far too late. It had probably been too late for her the first time she'd ever laid eyes on him. "To the right," she whispered weakly. "Watch out for the chair."

She'd changed the sheets when she'd cleaned her bedroom, and now they were going to get all sandy again. The irrelevant thought flickered through her mind and was lost as Rune lowered her onto the double bed. Pausing only long enough to shed his single garment, he followed her down.

Even the feel of his body heat was erotic. The night swim had cooled her skin, but it took only the incendiary touch of his hand on her waist to set off fire storms that robbed her lungs of air. A small sob emerged from her throat, and she felt herself being gathered against the lean, powerful strength of him.

"Corey, sweetheart, sweetheart, let me taste you again."

She felt the brush of his mustache, and then the cool, firm pressure of his closed lips, and she began to melt. He made no effort to deepen the kiss, although she could feel the rough tremors that coursed through his body.

Instead, he allowed the intimacy of the gentle contact to develop to its fullest, encouraging the participation of her fevered imagination until Corey could have screamed at his restraint.

Then, when her lips trembled against the need to devour him, he shifted, and she was brought into mind-shattering contact with the virile force of his masculinity. A sound like the whimper of an animal formed in her throat, and he captured it, parting her lips in a ravaging kiss of blatant sexuality.

One darkly textured leg crossed over her thighs, holding her captive. With the fingers of one hand tangled in her hair, he used the other to conquer proud summits, to explore soft, subtle plains and hidden valleys, leaving devastation and need behind him wherever he went.

The scent of the sea was all around them, clinging to overheated flesh, to the sun-dried linens beneath them. Corey raked trembling fingers through his springy curls, glorying in their vitality, and then her hands moved down to trace the pattern of resilient hair that spread across his broad chest, that narrowed as it swept downward, only to broaden once more on his hard, flat abdomen.

She heard the air whistle in through his teeth and snatched back her hand.

"Don't stop now," he ground out. He took her wrist and guided it, falling back onto the pillow with a soft moan as her hesitant hand closed around him. "Ah, great glory," he sighed, and then, abruptly, he caught her hand up and carried it to his lips, kissing each finger in turn. When the smallest one slipped into his mouth, to be stroked by his tongue, nibbled by his teeth, Corey stiffened.

"Don't be frightened, sweetheart," he whispered, lowering his face to her throat. A series of slow kisses followed an exquisitely sensitive trail down the side of her neck as his hands advanced to prepare the way. Gathering one breast into a small cone, he took its erect tip into his mouth, coercing it with his tongue until she was writhing in ecstasy beneath him.

Then his hand moved unerringly through the darkness to close over the silken thatch that joined her trembling thighs. Her hips recoiled in an instinctive attempt to escape his compelling touch.

"Easy, love, slow and easy," Rune murmured, gentling her as he might have gentled one of his high-strung polo ponies. "Trust me, it's all right. Let me make it wonderful for you."

His hands were already making it wonderful for her, and Corey felt herself arching to meet his stroking touch. It was *too* wonderful. It was all she'd ever dreamed it could be, all she'd ever hoped for so long ago, before the disappointment of reality had set in.

"I don't think—" she began, as doubt flickered dimly.

"That's right, don't think." He took her head between his hands and began kissing her—her eyes, her cheeks, the corners of her mouth. Then, with a groan, he took her lips and moved to a position above her.

It was far too late to turn back. It had been too late forever. Corey, with her heart pounding at her throat, felt the wonderful weight of him settle between her thighs, and she rose to meet him. With a wisdom born of the ages rather than her own limited experience, she remained quiescent until the last possible moment. Then, when ring after ring of sharp pleasure surrounded her, blazing with light and color, she joined in the full, glorious fury of the storm, vocalizing in a way that would have mortified her if she'd even been conscious of it.

Uttering one deep, ragged cry, Rune collapsed, taking care to spare her the full weight of his body. Dimly, she realized that even as they'd raced toward the summit, he'd never left her. She hadn't known that a man could be so generous.

"How are we doing down there?" he asked, his voice husky with an emotion she couldn't begin to interpret. "Need some air?"

She needed to hang on to him more than she needed air, but she didn't know how to tell him. She had a feeling he wouldn't welcome any hint of clinging, even now. Words drifted in and out of her mind, words she instinctively rejected. Love words.

They hadn't spoken any. Even if he'd said them to her, she'd have known he was lying. But what about her? What about the feeling that had led her to this? Love? How could it be? It was too soon. She didn't particularly care for the alternatives, but it *couldn't* be love.

"Wake me up for breakfast, will you?" she murmured. Sleep was safe, and much, much kinder than her own remorseful conscience. She'd wrestle with that tomorrow.

The rattling hum of a compressor cutting in woke Rune, and he opened his eyes, instantly alert. The sound of soft breathing beside him took only a moment to register, and he turned his head on the unfamiliar pillow and inhaled the subtle sea-washed fragrance of her.

Corey. He mouthed the words silently. How incredibly sweet she'd been, half-shy, half-wanton, letting him take the lead as though that were the only thing she knew. How long had she said she'd been married? Half her life? What the devil had she been married to?

Slipping out of bed without disturbing her, Rune felt for his trunks. They were sandy and clammy, unpleasant against his skin, but he pulled them on and then he let himself out, closing the door silently. Before he faced her again he had some serious thinking to do. He also needed a shower, a shave, and some clean, dry clothes.

Dawn was a thin slice of light stretched tautly across the horizon. The power was back on; maybe the phones would be, too. As soon as it was late enough, Rune knew he'd have to call his mother and let her know he was all right. Some of the Raleigh news stations could have mentioned the waterspout.

The phone was ringing when he let himself into his cottage. Swearing at the drifts of sand that banked the floors, he crossed to answer it. They'd shoveled out most of Corey's place before dark. He'd have to tackle his now.

"Toad? How're you doing, old fellow?" he greeted softly as he passed the covered cage. Then he snatched up the receiver to hear his mother's voice, shrill with worry.

"Rune? Thank the Lord! I've been trying to get through all night long, ever since I heard it on the late news. Are you all right? They said it went through a relatively undeveloped stretch of Emerald Isle, and as far as I know, Abbie's is about the most undeveloped. Are you all right? Were you there when it happened? Is Abbie's cousin all right? I'd better try to get in touch with Abbie—no, I don't suppose she'd hear about it over in Zurich, or wherever she is, so best not to worry her.

And then, after a moment of leaden silence, "Rune? Are you still there? This dratted phone system—hello! *Hello!*"

Rune replaced the phone and then deliberately took it off the hook. Moving slowly, almost as if he were underwater, he crossed the room and lifted the cover from the three-by-five-foot cage. Then he prowled, feet gritting unpleasantly on the aftermath of the storm. Finally, he crossed to the phone again. He may as well get it over with—otherwise he'd have her on his neck before the sun was even up. It wouldn't be the first time she'd chartered a helicopter when ordinary means weren't fast enough to suit her. The first two times he dialed, he got a busy signal. With bleak determination, he persisted.

"Mother? No, we didn't get cut off, I hung up on you. Look, I'm all right. The spout passed between the cottages, but no one was hurt and the damage was superficial. Now, would you mind telling me just how the hell you knew where I was, and how you came to know about Abigail Murchison? You set me up again, didn't you?"

"Now, Rune, don't go all cold and courtroomy on me. There's one thing I learned from your father: never allow yourself to be cross-examined if you can possibly get out of it. Either you come across as hiding something, or you end up saying things that don't really need to be said."

"Just answer two questions." A pale gray light was beginning to spill through the windows. It matched Rune's mood precisely.

"Then, stop leading your witness. I've known Abbie for years, since my first term on the school board.

Naturally when I happened to run into her after you'd rented her place, she mentioned it."

"And Corey?"

"Well, we might have discussed—"

"Thanks, Mother." The bitterness was unmistakable, but at least it disguised the pain, the damned debilitating self-disgust he was feeling. "Remind me to share a joke with you someday."

After watching the sky turn from tarnished silver to a clear heat-washed blue, Rune stirred himself into action. A call to a garage in Swansboro, and another one to Judge Burrus came first. Toad was still backed into a corner, doggedly plucking the feathers from his ragged breast, and Rune carefully removed him from the cage long enough to clean it. That done, and the amenities taken care of, he returned the unnaturally silent bird to the security of his custom-built cage, all the time carrying on a low, reassuring monologue.

God! He felt anything but reassuring. He felt like throwing something. He felt like *breaking* something! Corey's small tanned neck, for starters. How could he have been such a damned gullible fool? She'd as good as told him what she was. They'd even joked about it, for cripe's sake!

Some joke. He'd actually begun to entertain ideas of asking her to marry him even before last night. Fortunately, he'd learned a long time ago never to act on an emotional impulse. Give it time, and once the emotion's drained away, if there's anything left, look it over in a good, strong light. Then, if action is called for, act.

Well, he'd acted, all right, but thank God he hadn't committed the ultimate blunder. It would serve her right if he led her all the way up the garden path and then dumped her where it would hurt the most.

She was good, though. He'd have to hand it to her. She'd had him convinced that she was down here simply to pull herself together after a divorce and consider her next move. And all the time, she'd known exactly what her next move was going to be. Rune McLaughlin. That was her next move. Number one on the hit parade of eligible Southern men. "And if you play your cards right, ladies," Rune jeered derisively, "a lifetime mealticket can be yours for only a small initial investment. Step right up, take a chance. What have you got to lose?"

Hell, she'd probably been rehearsing her act ever since Abigail had tipped her off that there was a hot prospect all set up for her.

If there were any flaws in his case, they didn't occur to him as he went through the motions of showering and dressing. By the time the wrecker had come, he'd closed his mind, secured the cottage, and was ready to go pick up his car. The game was over.

Remembrance came with a rush, before she'd even opened her eyes. Corey wriggled one foot across the bed. It met with no resistance, no hard, warm flesh, and she flopped over and opened her eyes, blinking at the sunlight that poured in through the screened window. Then she sat up, yawning and rubbing sleep-swollen eyes.

From the looks of it, she'd slept the morning away. "Rune?" she croaked experimentally. Grimacing, she eased out of the bed, immediately aware of the stiffness of her thighs, the tenderness of certain other portions of her body.

Ye gods, she'd really done it. If anyone had told her a month ago that she'd find herself falling head over heels in love with a man she'd just met, she'd have laughed hysterically.

Instead, the laugh was on her. In love she might be—in love she undoubtedly *was*, to have allowed last night to happen—but that didn't automatically mean that Rune returned her feelings. Even if he did, he'd told her how he felt about marriage. Of course, they could live together. Lots of couples did these days. Generations of her ancestors would be revolving in their graves at the very idea, but if she had to choose between that or losing him, there was no contest.

With one foot in the tub, she paused in the job of adjusting the water temperature, a dreamy smile softening her features. What was it he'd said? That he hadn't known how much she was going to mean to him? For a man like Rune, that was tantamount to an admission, wasn't it? Attractive, successful professional men in his age bracket would have learned to be chary of outright declarations. His being a lawyer would make him even more so.

Edwin had declared his love in the tenth grade, and from then on, with every means at his disposal, he'd waged a constant battle to get her to sleep with him, including clumsily worded love letters and frequent impassioned, if inarticulate, pleas. She could count on one hand the times he'd mentioned the word *love* after they were married.

It was good to get clean again, with soap and shampoo and talcum and dry underwear. So far, it was relatively cool, but the day would heat up quickly, and they still had a lot of dirty work to do.

"But tonight . . ." Smiling, she allowed her mind to drift over all the wonderful possibilities as she let herself out the backdoor and hurried across to Rune's cottage. She'd been rather surprised to find him gone when she'd woken up, but he'd probably wanted the same things she had, a bath and a change of clothes.

And of course, he might have wanted to get an early start so they could finish up quicker.

"Rune, have you had breakfast?" she called out as she ran up the steps. The door clattered behind her and she wrinkled her nose at the untouched mounds of sand, the overturned chair, the torn screen. "Rune? Are you there?"

Maybe he was still showering and couldn't hear her. She called again. "Rune? Rune, are you in there?"

Surely he wouldn't have gone swimming without her, Corey thought as puzzlement gave way to disquiet. The windows were open, the shutters hooked back, but the back door was closed.

She frowned. To her knowledge, he'd never closed it before. "Rune?" Her voice had lost some of its bright expectancy by now. Before her hand even touched the knob, she knew what she'd find.

9

As the day crept on with no sign of Rune, Corey's emotions plunged blindly down an all-too-familiar path. The disbelief came first. Something vitally important must have come up suddenly, she told herself as she collected the used towels and tossed them into the hamper. Even so, surely he would have had time to jot a few words on a scrap of paper and stick it in her screen door. Surely by now he'd have found a minute to call.

Next came the outrage. How *dare* he go off and leave her without a word? Did he have to make it quite so plain that she was of no more interest to him now? It had been the challenge, of course. A man like Rune wouldn't be accustomed to resistance from a woman. He'd persisted until she'd given in, and then he'd deliberately taken this way of proving to her that his precious freedom was still intact.

Men. Damned hunters, every one of them. They could no more help chasing women than Jack could help chasing birds. And a hunter, Corey reminded herself grimly, didn't continue to stalk his prey once he'd captured it.

Anger ebbed, to be replaced by a brief flurry of self-pity. Corey allowed herself to wallow lugubriously for the space of a few minutes. Once a victim, always a victim, she lamented. Rune had introduced her to a world of incredible pleasure and promptly deserted her, leaving her to rattle in the wind like a dried gourd, filled with the seeds of faded memories.

"Bull," she muttered succinctly. She had a clothesline to replace, and here she was wasting time weeping over a man who wasn't worth the salt of a single tear. If she had to weep, she could weep for two dish towels, a set of sheets, and a beautiful yellow linen dress, never mind that it had to be washed and ironed after every wearing.

Exit self-pity, enter guilt. Oh, she knew all the stages, all right. If there was one thing she was an expert in, it was the role of rejectee. Only what she'd gone through before had been nothing compared to the anguish she felt now. A mixture of physical pain and grief, the fact that she'd brought it on herself didn't make it any easier to bear.

If only she'd leveled with him from the start instead of pretending to be someone she wasn't, he'd have left her alone and none of this would have happened. He'd as good as admitted—in fact he'd made a point of informing her—that she wasn't the sort of woman who normally attracted him.

Rune had all those lofty degrees. He knew which wine went with what and quoted things she'd never heard of.

She had an associate degree in art, knew which brand of peanut butter was the best buy, and if she quoted anything, it would probably be Dr. Seuss or one of the few classics she could remember from high school. She was strictly a small-town product without a sophisticated bone in her body: not outstandingly smart, not particularly young, and not particularly pretty, in spite of an expensive raid on St. Louis's best shopping mall. And she'd been fluttering around like a silly girl, pretending for all she was worth that she wasn't trembling on the brink of grandmotherhood.

Look at Granny Peters in her string bikini. What was Granny doing on the beach with that man, Mama? Corey's hyperactive imagination was off and running again. With a soft moan, she pointed the garden hose toward the pool and turned it on in an effort to drown out the vivid image.

Hours later, wrapped in a beach towel against the evening coolness, she sat on top of the dune, took another gulp of the raw red wine and made a face. She'd made a grandiose gesture of pouring out the champagne Rune had given her, which left her with the jug of imported stuff he'd scorned.

Rather fitting, she thought. If only it were a little more palatable, she could enjoy the irony still more.

"A modest little paint thinner with an ingenuous hint of raw sewage," she mocked. Still, if it had any anesthetic properties, it was worth it.

Scorned. Rejected. The story of her life, Corey thought dolefully.

Twisting around, she scowled at the sound of a noisy vehicle out on the highway. Sighing in disappointment, she resumed her task of watching the tide come in. She'd overseen its egress, waited patiently during the slack period, and now she was supervising its return.

He *could* have left her a note. When she'd first noticed that the truck was missing, she'd assumed that he'd taken it to a garage to have the windshield replaced, but that would hardly have taken all day.

With exaggerated care, she poured herself another glass of wine. If he hadn't locked his darned door, she'd have raided his kitchen for the bottle he'd promised her. He'd promised her a lot of things, she reminded herself with a slightly bleary return of self-pity. The one thing he hadn't promised was to love, honor, and obey.

Or was that supposed to be her line? It had been so long, she'd forgotten.

"Nobody obeys anyone these days," she complained to the boldest of the ghost crabs that had been studying her curiously with their stalklike eyes. "And promises?" she snorted. "Promises don't mean doodlesquat anymore. Here's to you, my tall-eyed friends. Rose gardens forever." Sitting cross-legged on the top of the dune, Corey waved her glass, and the crabs suddenly disappeared as if by magic.

The low growl of a powerful engine grew louder and then ceased altogether. Corey, intent on luring the crabs from their burrows, didn't hear it. "Here, crabbie, crabbie. Come out and play with Corey."

A low beam of light swept over the base of the dune before being extinguished. Oblivious, she leaned forward from the hips and planted her elbows in the sand. "Please come back, li'l crabbies. Don't run away from Corey. Nice crabbie, come on out now; Granny Corey'll tell you a nursery rhyme."

Waving her wineglass like a faulty metronome, she began to chant. "This li'l crabbie went to market, this li'l crabbie stayed home; this li'l crabbie had roast beef, this li'l—"

"Would you mind telling me just what the hell you think you're doing?"

The familiar low voice crackled down her spine, causing Corey to spill half her wine onto the sand. She lurched up from her elbows, swaying only slightly, and twisted around to stare up at the tall figure looming over her.

Gone was the Rune of the casual clothes, the shaggy, sun-bleached bronze curls, the bushy mustache that caressed and tickled and softened the edges of his kisses. In his place stood a flawlessly groomed stranger, his long limbs sheathed in some crisp, dark fabric, his chest, that same chest she'd bruised with her nose just yesterday, covered in pristine white.

Carefully, she arranged her legs in a manner slightly less inelegant, took a long, fortifying swallow from her wineglass, searched her mind for a quotation on treachery, and intoned accusingly, "Tee hee, Brute?"

It was hard to judge Rune's reaction to her newfound erudition, especially as her eyes seemed to have anchored themselves somewhere in the vicinity of his navel and refused to budge an inch in any direction.

"I beg your pardon?" he repeated slowly.

"It's a quote," Corey informed him haughtily. "You're not the only one who can quote quotes, you know."

"Would you care to name your source?"

Corey riffled clumsily through her repertoire. Unfortunately, spanning the distance between Mother Goose and William Shakespeare took a bit more concentration than she could muster at the moment. "Well, it's *not* from Para—Parsel—Paralysis!"

Rune's hands, when he relieved her of her glass and helped her to her feet, were almost gentle. His voice, when he cautioned her against tripping over the wine jug, trembled on a deeper note that could have been anger or laughter.

Of the two, Corey preferred his anger. She was in the mood for a good, air-cleansing fight. "Would you *mind?*" she seethed indignantly, jerking her arm from his grasp and then staggering in the soft sand to regain her balance.

Somehow, Rune managed to steer her back to the cottage. He was sorely tempted to throw her over his shoulder, dump her across her bed, and leave her there, wet, sandy, and soused to the gills. Lord knows she didn't deserve any better. On the other hand, his conscience had been giving him a few bad moments. In a way, he'd been as guilty as she was. Having lied about his own background, he was not in an ideal position to cast any stones.

Of course, his only motive had been self-protection. Hers had been something considerably less admirable.

On the screened porch, Rune removed the sandy beach towel from her fists and went to work on her damp, rumpled clothes. She was wearing those white pajama things again. He located the diagonal zipper and tugged it down ruthlessly. "You didn't go swimming alone, did you?" he demanded.

"I don' think tha's any concern of yours," Corey mumbled self-righteously. Actually, she'd been trying to

146

secure the hose in the bottom of the pool with a brick when it had turned on her. Rather than spend the next few days holding it, she'd decided to have a civilized drink while she communed with nature.

"Stay out of the ocean. It can be slick as glass one day and treacherous as the devil the next, and you can't always judge the danger by surface appearances."

And that's the damned truth, Rune reminded himself with bitter cynicism, propping her waist against his shoulder as he knelt to lift her bare feet from the damp, wadded pants legs. Sand was embedded in her skin from her feet to the top of her head. She must have been rolling in it. Unless he missed his guess, she was in for one hell of a miserable night.

"Well?" Corey demanded, struggling to control eyelids that for some reason refused to stay up. "What have you got t' say for yourself?"

"Believe me, you wouldn't want to hear it." His hands itched to turn her over his knee and vent some of the anger that was all mixed up with disappointment and frustration. She acted as if *she* were the injured party.

"Sorry I didn' come up to your lof'y—lof-tee standards. Can't say I didn' warn you."

"You're drunk." Watching her fan those impossibly dense eyelashes, Rune felt something twist painfully inside him. "For what it's worth, I'm sorry, too," he admitted finally. There was a certain masochistic relief in speaking the words aloud. Fortunately, he was safe in the knowledge that she'd never remember them tomorrow.

Corey shrugged, an exaggerated motion that threatened to overbalance her. As they stood facing each other in the dim light, she braced herself against a wicker table and tried to look blasé—not an easy feat considering the fact that both her stomach and her head were beginning to turn on her.

It occurred to her belatedly that she was all but naked, and her hands fluttered ineffectually in front of her body. Why on earth had she ever been fool enough to throw out all her good white cotton underwear and replace it with these frothy little scraps of lace? Face it; she had a no-nonsense, one-hundred-percent-cotton personality, and after all these years, it was too late to change.

Utterly miserable, she tried to think of a polite way to bring this farce to an end. "Will that be all?" she blurted finally.

Rune stared at her silently until she cringed. Then he spat out a single expletive and wheeled away, slamming the screen door behind him.

Growing more painfully sober by the minute, Corey stared after him. Tears burned in her eyes, and she pushed them away with salty, sandy fists. And then she swore, too.

Back to the beginning. If Corey was determined to avoid Rune, he seemed equally determined to avoid her. If he drove off, she stayed at the cottage, but if his car remained in the driveway, she took off. Some days he came home while she was having her supper on the porch, and she used the shelter of the screen to gaze longingly at the easy way he had of moving as he loped up the steps, the proud set of his head as he jerked open the door and let it fall shut behind him.

He'd had his hair cut much shorter, but nothing could really tame those irrepressible curls. The carefully trimmed mustache was probably more appropriate for a successful lawyer, but Corey found she much preferred the shagginess of his beach bum days. Obviously, he was catering to someone else's tastes these days.

She was toying with her broiled shrimp late one evening when he drove up, and as always, she suffered a quick pang of fear that he wouldn't be alone. From her high vantage point she couldn't see into the passenger side of the car. He certainly seemed in no hurry to get out.

Imagination shifting into overdrive, Corey pictured him talking to a woman, the sort of woman *she'd* tried to become. They'd be laughing over some intimate little joke, and as he reached across to unclip her seat belt, his hands would linger to caress. Those strong, white teeth would flash in a smile, his eyes would sparkle like smoky topazes, and . . .

It occurred to Corey that she herself was probably the joke. He was probably telling his new girlfriend about the depressingly nice woman next door who'd turned out to be merely depressing.

Shoving her plate aside, Corey stood up and marched inside. So far she'd managed to avoid facing the truth of what was going on next door by seeing every movie for miles around and eating out at a different restaurant each night.

Well, damn it, she'd run out of movies, and she was sick of restaurant foods, whether broiled, panned in butter, fried, or au gratin. And furthermore, she was sick of being alone, with no one to talk to but a bored Jack.

"Sit down and be quiet, you moth-eaten old tomcat; I'm going to read to you," she threatened. Prowling the bookcases, she tugged a slender volume from the top shelf. *"The Old Man and the Sea,* by Ernest Hemingway," she announced belligerently. "It's about a fish; you'll love it."

Five minutes later she put the book down and sighed heavily. When was it supposed to start getting better? More to the point, where was her pride? How could she waste her time mooning over a lying, unprincipled scoundrel who lured women into falling in love with him and then, after he'd clipped their scalp to his belt, dropped them flat?

"Honestly, Jack, what woman would be fool enough to love a man like that? Don't answer that question." Sighing again—she did a lot of that these days—she allowed Jack to direct her feet to the kitchen cabinet where his food was kept.

During the following week she explored the surrounding country, taking one day trip after another, often not returning until long after dark. It was exhausting, but at least it enabled her to sleep. One of these days, when this raw, aching misery had faded, she'd probably go through all the brochures she'd collected and wish she'd paid more attention.

Dutifully, she called Winnie each Friday night. "Give me the measurements for the curtains and dust ruffle and tell me what colors you want," she instructed, feigning enthusiasm. Winnie had always hated sewing. At least Corey could do that much for her without running headlong into that blasted independent streak. "I hope you're taking your vitamins" was as close as she'd let herself come to maternal nagging.

"Don't worry, Mike counts 'em out to me every morning. We're doing the Lamaze thing, and Mike's the star pupil. Honestly, Mom, you'd think he was having this watermelon instead of me."

Her daughter seemed to have found herself that rarity, a decent man. If there was only one allotted per family, Corey was glad Winnie had him. She could handle unhappiness for herself, but not for her child.

After a day spent shopping for materials in Morehead City and New Bern, she turned into the driveway late one evening, hot, tired, and extremely hungry. To her dismay, Rune pulled in right behind her.

Corey fumbled with her purse and her packages, waiting for him to go inside. Instead, he sauntered around the hood of her car and braced his hand against the roof, blocking her way with that lean, powerful torso of his. He did it deliberately, she decided rancorously: the fitted knit shirt, the tight-fitting pants. Taunting her with what she was missing, no doubt. All she wanted was for him to move away so she could open her door.

Reluctantly, she unclipped her shoulder harness and flipped the latch, and Rune opened the door for her. "Been shopping, I see," he observed blandly.

"My, what keen eyes you have."

"My, what a sweet disposition you have."

"There's nothing wrong with my disposition. I simply don't see the point in stating the obvious." *Move, damn it, and let me by before I do something that will embarrass us both.*

"I hope you threw out the rest of that rank stuff you got sozzled on a few weeks ago."

"I did not get sozzled. I simply enjoyed a civilized glass of wine while I watched the tide come in—a perfectly reasonable pastime, surely."

"Perfectly," Rune agreed with a straight face. "And singing nursery rhymes to sand crabs is a perfectly reasonable pastime, too. Tell me, how was your headache the next day?"

"What headache?" Corey prevaricated. She'd had a four-alarm one, after waking up at daybreak to rid her system violently of all the wine she'd consumed. "I'm sure I haven't the faintest idea what you're getting at, so would you mind letting me get by?"

Rune considered shaking her until her teeth chattered. He'd hoped that after all this time, her effect on him would have worn off. He should have known better.

Look at her, he jeered to himself, as cool and innocent as a morning in May. There wasn't a judge or jury in the world that would be immune to those limpid gray eyes of hers.

Oh, he'd let her get by, all right. He'd almost let her get by with making a royal fool of him. If it hadn't been for that call from his mother, he'd have had the ring on her finger by now. Signed, sealed, and delivered.

With a mocking smile, he stepped back. "Sure, anything for a lady. I hope I haven't been disturbing you too much with my late nights. Figured my social life was overdue a little attention."

"Really? I hadn't noticed. I've been rather busy lately."

With a mocking look that suggested that he knew precisely how busy she'd been, Rune turned away.

"Oh, blast and damnation," Corey whispered hopelessly to herself. Gazing bleakly at his retreating back, she wondered how long she could stick it out.

She'd promised Abbie, though. And to be brutally honest with herself, she knew running away wouldn't solve a thing. There was no leaving behind a hurt of this magnitude. She could only try to outlast it.

The following night, Corey considered reconsidering that stand. Rune brought a woman back to the cottage with him. The car radio announced their arrival. Next came the slamming of two car doors, and then a burst of laughter that made Corey's fists tighten painfully. She'd spent a quiet day sewing. Now that it was finally cool enough to enjoy the screened porch, it looked as though she was fated to spend the evening listening to a wild party next door.

When the music started, she crumpled her napkin and stomped into the house. Surely there was an ordinance against that sort of carrying on. People had a right to a little peace and quiet, even here at the beach. *Especially* here at the beach.

Under the heat of a floor lamp, she scowled at the unlined panel curtains she'd been making for the nursery and discovered that two of the edges were hemmed on the wrong side. She had it all to rip out and do over, and it served her right for being such a blind, stupid fool. Weren't people supposed to learn from experience? Unfortunately, there were no remedial classes for people with her particular learning disability.

The laughter and music had been bad enough, but later on, when she could hear nothing at all, Corey stared at the gay cotton print in her lap until the yellow rabbits with their foolish little smiles all blurred together on their gingham meadows.

She *wouldn't* cry. An aching throat and a chin that insisted on quivering did *not* constitute crying.

* * *

The roses were delivered late the next day just as Corey was struggling to light a mound of charcoal in the grill. "Are you sure they're for me?" Wiping her blackened fingertips on her shorts, she took the long florists' box and examined it curiously for a card.

"If your name's Corey Peters they are," the black-haired boy in the muscleman T-shirt assured her.

"Just a minute," she murmured, "let me go get my purse."

With an engagingly regretful grin, the delivery boy told her it was all taken care of, and she thanked him and hurried inside to locate a vase. Red roses, a whole dozen of them, with the dew still on them. Who on earth—?

"Move over, Jack, let me look under that counter."

It had to be Winnie. On the other hand, why should her daughter be sending her flowers? It was too early for the baby to be here. It wasn't Mother's Day, it wasn't her birthday, and the curtains weren't even finished yet.

A thought occurred to her and she dismissed it out of hand. The last man on earth who'd be sending her red roses was Rune McLaughlin. Unless it was his way of offering her a belated apology. A sop for his guilty conscience? That would be the day! Besides, if he had the slightest inkling of what red roses were supposed to signify, he'd have made it ragweed.

Settling for a mason jar, she put the roses on the table and hurried outside to see if her charcoal, through some miracle, had decided to burn. She was just in time to see the delivery boy skip down Rune's steps two at a time, leap into his van and roar off.

"I don't believe it," she murmured slowly. "So it *was*

Rune." She couldn't begin to guess at his motive, but whatever it was, she wasn't going to make the same mistake twice. If he had anything to say to her, he could say it with words, not with the ambiguous language of flowers.

From the shelter of his screened porch, Rune clutched the long-stemmed red roses that had just been delivered and stared out at the woman on the dune. She was wasting matches again, trying to light three pounds of charcoal to grill half a pound of beef. Probably waiting for him to come out and help her.

Red roses, no less, he mused. He'd say this for her: She didn't go in for halfway measures. First the champagne, now this. He shook his head in grudging admiration. He'd been playing the game for some twenty-five years, and she was about as skilled an operator as he'd ever run across. She knew precisely when to advance and when to retreat. She dangled her innocuous bait, and if he showed any sign of interest, she turned those remarkable eyes on him and . . .

And the truth was, he'd fallen for it. He was used to dealing with all sorts of women—playgirls, socialites, professional women. He even found himself fending off the occasional ingenue, and what's more, he fancied he did it with commendable finesse.

What he *hadn't* expected to meet was a beguiling combination of all these types. A woman who'd been oddly sheltered in some ways, badly injured in others. A woman who was intelligent and capable without being abrasive about it, warm and witty in a perfectly natural way. A woman, he added dryly, with damned few marketable job skills.

He shrugged as an unpleasant thought occurred to him. Was that why she did it? After having a man to support her all those years, did she figure it was still the best bet?

God help him, Rune thought bleakly, he was in love with her.

It was an impossible situation, of course. After avoiding that particular pitfall all his life, he'd be a fool to marry a woman who'd deliberately set out to trap him, especially since it had been for all the wrong reasons. If they'd met before, and she'd fallen for him and decided to try her luck . . .

No. There was no way he could pretend it didn't matter. His self-respect couldn't take it, even if his ego survived.

All right, so he'd made a serious mistake. Admitting it was the first step on the road to recovery. Forget revenge. Forget everything but getting himself out of this thing with a whole skin.

Wheeling around, Rune snatched up the long-stemmed roses, swearing fiercely as thorns pierced his skin in several places. With brutal disregard for their dew-fresh innocence, he crammed them into the trash can and slammed the lid on them.

That should do for starters. First thing tomorrow he'd get the hell out of here. He could pack up and be gone by ten . . . except for Toad.

Again he swore as a feeling of frustration tightened the muscles at the back of his neck. When he'd moved down for the summer, he'd rented a trailer and hauled the large cage, using a carrier for transporting the bird. So all right, he'd get a later start. At least he'd get out of here before he did anything monumentally stupid. Like forgetting what he knew about her and taking what she offered.

When Rune left to pick up Gayle, whose last name he still couldn't recall after three dates, Corey was grilling her supper. It would be cooked to the consistency of shoe leather and served with wilted lettuce and bottled dressing, he predicted scornfully.

"And face it, McLaughlin," he growled as he slid under the wheel and slammed the door with unnecessary force, "you'd trade six Gayle whoozits for the chance to share it with her."

No, it wasn't going to be easy. It hadn't taken long to discover that they were in complete harmony in most areas, disagreeing just enough to add spice to their discussions. There were so many things he'd loved to have taught her, things she could have taught him . . . things they could have shared. He'd even looked forward to springing her on his mother. He'd been so damned proud of her, and that was the most ironic part of all.

God, he'd give everything he owned if only she hadn't come down here for the express purpose of entrapping him, and then lied about it. She'd even had the gall to confess, doing it in such a way that he hadn't really taken her seriously. Clever woman.

All during an interminable evening with the woman he'd picked up at a bar several nights before, Rune did his best to direct his thoughts to the topic she seemed to find most fascinating. He was not particularly interested in which female soap star was sleeping with which male one, but he nodded and managed an occasional monosyllabic response.

Three drinks into the evening, his conscience was

goading him again. Corey had lied, but so had he. By omission, if not directly. Was her deception really all that much worse than his?

Gayle seemed disappointed when Rune declined her invitation for a nightcap. "Is your back bothering you again?" she asked, running her hand over the area in question. She was a big girl, a tall, well-built blonde who seemed to be on an extended vacation at one of the more expensive hotels on the beach. She had an unfortunate tendency to lapse into baby talk at unexpected moments, although Rune seriously doubted that it was a case of his bringing out the maternal instinct in her.

Not at all proud of himself, Rune mumbled something about an expected business call. You're getting to be an old hand at double-dealing, McLaughlin.

"A business call at this time of night?" Gayle said skeptically. Gold charm bracelet jangling noisily, she dropped her hand from his shoulder.

Rune had the grace to look embarrassed. The night before, he'd made some excuse about a riding accident, hinting delicately that it had rendered him temporarily at a disadvantage. The accident was no lie, only it had happened four years before, and he'd been out of action for all of two weeks.

Before he'd left the hotel parking lot, he'd forgotten the existence of the woman with whom he'd spent three interminable evenings. By the time he'd left Morehead City for the beach strand, he was as thoroughly ensnared as ever by a pair of hauntingly lovely, if damnably perfidious, gray eyes.

10

The trouble was, he couldn't make himself simply drive off and forget he'd ever heard of a woman named Corey Peters. Rune had packed his belongings, stacked his luggage in the living room, and cleaned Toad's traveling cage. And then he'd alternately brooded and paced, now and then pausing to glare out through the darkness at the cottage next door.

Forget her? Who the devil had he been kidding? Regardless of how they'd met, he was hooked. If he called it a summer and went back to Raleigh now, it would be like ripping out his soul and leaving it behind. For the past two days, morning and afternoon, he'd watched her march past the pool, trudge across the powdery dune, and wade out into the ocean as if she'd been doing it all her life. And he'd skulked in here like a craven coward, afraid to simply walk out there and tell her how he felt. A victim of that stiff-necked pride he'd worn like a badge of honor all these years. Hell, he'd even been proud of his pride.

She'd looked so small, so achingly vulnerable. If there'd been even the slightest sign of an undertow, if it hadn't been clear as a bathtub and almost as calm, he'd have yanked her out of there pronto.

He'd had to keep reminding himself that she was of age. If she chose to swim alone, it was her own affair. God save the queen, hadn't she proved conclusively that she was more than capable of looking out for herself?

Rune felt as though he were being physically pulled apart by all this business. Swearing under his breath, he smacked a hard fist into the palm of his other hand. Damn it all, it was time he stopped equivocating and got down to the basics. If she thought she could twist him around her little finger from here on out, she had a few things to learn. And he was just about in the proper frame of mind to start teaching lesson number one.

As for the way it had all started, he could rise above that. It hadn't been easy, but he'd rationalized the business with his mother to the point where he could stomach it. He'd concede the first round—with the understanding that it did not establish a precedent. Oh, they were guilty, no question of it, right up to their ever-loving eyebrows—conspiracy, collusion, intent to deceive. All three of them, Abigail included, could give lessons to the best con artist in the business.

Well, he wasn't a small-minded man. Having known his mother all these years, he could understand someone like Corey falling under her influence. When Helen McLaughlin wanted something badly enough, she went after it with the dedication and directness of an M-1 Abrams tank.

Yeah, the more he thought of it, the surer he was that it could work. If you can't lick 'em, join 'em, he rationalized. He owed it to his fellow bachelors to break up the conspiracy, to account for at least one of the collaborators.

The cool, analytical part of Rune's mind nodded sagely. Sure, old man, and as long as you can hang on to the belief that that's your sole reason for marrying her, you might even stand a chance of surviving.

Corey squinted her eyes and rethreaded the needle. She was determined to finish what she'd started, and then she'd mail the whole bundle off to Winnie, find a boarding kennel for Jack, and go somewhere else. Anywhere else. She'd had enough of this island paradise to last her a lifetime.

Sniffling, she fumbled for a tissue, hoping she wasn't coming down with a cold. Summer colds were the very pits, and her resistance was bound to be lower than usual. She hadn't been sleeping at all well, and her appetite had dropped off to nothing.

And as if that weren't enough, there was all that dumb swimming. Scared stiff, she'd made herself stay out there every day until she was shivering with cold and her fingers resembled bleached prunes. All the time, of course, she'd carefully kept her eyes averted from Rune's cottage.

He'd been at home. She knew every time he set foot out of his house; knew to the minute just how long he was gone. He'd been the one who'd cautioned her against swimming alone, but evidently, those warnings no longer applied. He hadn't bothered to join her. He hadn't even bothered to chew her out for disregarding his advice, and that had really hurt.

When the roses had come, she'd hoped . . .

Corey bit her lip and whipped the needle through the soft fabric. Since then, he'd completely ignored her, and now she was so confused she didn't know *what* to think. If that had been his idea of an apology, why bother? She'd much rather have had his friendship, if that was all he could offer. A dozen roses and then . . . nothing. Zilch.

Damn it, she couldn't be bought that cheaply. What had happened between them had been as much his fault as hers, and if he'd changed his mind afterward and was embarrassed now by the whole thing, then that was his problem.

Reaching the end of her thread again, Corey nipped it viciously with her teeth and then shook the panel out and examined it. Just lately the thought of holding an infant in her arms after all these years had been having a remarkably mellowing effect on her. Even now, she felt her anger begin to ebb, to be replaced by a feeling of warmth. There were worse fates than becoming a grandmother at thirty-seven.

The pale green and yellow bunny print was perfect, and she hadn't been able to resist buying half a yard of batiste of each of several pastel colors. She'd already completed three of the sleeveless shirts Winnie had lived in the summer she was born. Of course, this would be a winter baby, but even so . . .

Reaching for one of the tiny diaper shirts she'd spread out over the back of the sofa, she held it up and admired her handiwork. The yellow rabbits she'd embroidered down the front looked a little like inebriated groundhogs, but who cared? Everyone would be too busy admiring her beautiful granddaughter to notice what she wore.

The screen door slammed, and still holding the infant-size shirt, Corey glanced up. When Rune appeared suddenly in the doorway, she crumpled it in her lap and stared at him, unable to prevent the look of sheer joy from lighting her face.

The tableau held for the space of a few moments. Afterward, it seemed to Corey as though she'd held her breath for a year. There was all the time in the world to notice that his hair was shaggy again, that he was wearing a disreputable pair of jeans, and that his feet were bare. And that he looked more wonderful to her than ever, in spite of a certain grayness about his face, the deep lines that slashed across his brow, and a widening look of shock in his hazel eyes as he looked at the mounds of baby clothes.

"Rune," she murmured softly. Her smile hopelessly out of control, Corey shoved her sewing aside and jumped up to greet him. Tiny pastel shirts tumbled carelessly onto bunny printed curtains. Arms already lifted in welcome, she watched in stunned disbelief as he whirled around and stormed out. By the time the screen door slammed noisily behind him, one shockingly crude word still trembled in the air.

"Of all the calculating—" Rune toppled the rusted grill with a well-aimed kick as he strode across the gritty concrete. "I don't *believe* this! She's out of her cunning little mind to think she can get away with pulling a stunt like that!"

Limping, he let himself into his own cottage and headed for the liquor cabinet. He poured himself a stiff drink, downed it, and then poured another one. "What the hell kind of an idiot does she think I am? Any first year biology student knows better than that!"

Sprawled in a chair in the darkened room several minutes later, he stared broodingly out at the streak of moonlight that beat a narrow silver path to the shore. To think he'd credited her with a modicum of intelligence, not to mention common decency. What the devil did she take him for? The dumbest hick knew it didn't work that fast.

"One quick tumble, and a few weeks later she's preparing me for the blessed event? Come on, lady, give me a break!" he snarled into his whiskey.

The scent of bruised and fading roses slipped through his guard to affront him still further. Late the night before in a weak moment, he'd resurrected them from the garbage can. Well, he had a better idea. On his way out of town, he'd give the damned things back to her.

"With a polite note of thanks for the ride," he muttered with bitter satisfaction.

The twenty-one-year-old Scotch settled uncomfortably in his stomach, reminding him that he hadn't eaten recently. Recklessly, he emptied his glass and reached for the bottle.

A distasteful thought occurred to him. Maybe both he *and* his mother had been set up. If she'd had a bun in the oven all along, she might have figured this was as good a way as any to kill a couple of birds with one stone.

"Feather her nest, so to speak," he added, pleased with his brilliant trio of clichés. He frowned as a minor flaw in his reasoning occurred to him. She'd already been here more than a month. If she'd known she was pregnant when she'd arrived, that would make her at least three months along. Surely she didn't expect to pull a stunt like that and get away with it.

But there was Emmy Disher. Rune's frown deepened into a scowl. Abe had sworn that his wife could tell when she was one-week pregnant by a list of symptoms so bizarre as to be unbelievable. Still, there was the indisputable fact that Abe had predicted the birth of all three of his sons eight-and-a-half months before the fact.

"Crap," Rune muttered, draining his glass again. Rising unsteadily to his feet, he uncovered Toad's cage. He felt an obscure need to unburden himself, and Toad was not only discreet, he was available.

"Toad, old man, did it ever occur to you that man's best friend is not necessarily of the canine persuasion?"

The parrot bobbed his head and regarded him with an unblinking orange-rimmed gaze.

"I don't happen to speak Portuguese, sport, but you get my drift. First thing I'm going to do when we get home is to find you a parrottess. If you know what's good for you, you'll take her as is, warts and all, because none of us is perfect, m'friend."

Weaving slightly on his bare feet, he stared solemnly at the molting, ill-tempered yellow-naped Amazon. "And now that I've had time to peruse the matter a little more fully, I don't believe I'd care to live with a genuine paragon, would you? Perfection can get pretty damned tedious. Perfection, ol' Toad, ol' man, might draw the line at sharing her nest with a raunchy old coot who sheds his vest every time he gets nervous."

"Rune? Aré you there?"

Rune staggered and tripped over his stacked luggage, landing hard on his butt. God save the queen, she'd followed him home.

"Go away, damn it, I'm not ready to talk to you yet!" Untangling his uncoordinated limbs, he got to his feet and carefully restacked the luggage. Should have put the damned stuff in his car as soon as he'd packed it. Should have—

"Rune?"

He turned, moving with exaggerated care. The voice was disconcertingly like Corey's, but he could have sworn it had come from the parrot's jagged beak. How many doubles had he jolted down in the past half-hour?

"Corey?" he called out suspiciously, never taking his eyes from the ragged green and yellow parrot.

"Rune, are you there?"

It was Toad, all right. "Where the devil d'you learn that trick, you sadistic old crow?"

"*Corvo louco,*" Toad chortled. "*Corvo sujo.*"

Thoroughly shaken, Rune yanked the cover over the cage. Had she actually come looking for him, calling his name that way? The thought gave him a swift visceral kick. He could picture her calling through the door, through the windows, her soft little voice growing more and more puzzled as she padded from window to window outside his cottage.

"God, where's your brain, man? The woman's a flimflam artist. And you," he glared blearily at the parrot, "you poor dumb turkey, you fell for her." Lifting his voice to a ludicrous falsetto, he called, "Roo—oon." He'd long ago given up on getting so much as a simple hello from his Portuguese-speaking pet. There must be some truth in what he'd always heard—that a parrot would often pick up words spoken by a woman simply because of the higher pitch of her voice.

"Crazy, stinking old bundle of feathers," he grumbled, dropping into a chair beside the window that looked out over Corey's cottage.

Her lights were off. He was tempted to go back over there and drag her out of bed and get the damned truth out of her, but after the way that booze had hit his empty stomach, he'd probably wind up falling into the swimming pool.

No, better wait until morning. He was about to commit the ultimate premeditated folly, and for that he needed a clear head.

Grimly determined to finish the dust ruffle before she left, Corey was up early. She cooked herself an egg and stared at it gloomily while she sipped coffee. Then she tipped it into Jack's dish, opened the door and called him in off the top step, where he slept.

One harried glance around the house told her that it would probably take more than a single day to get ready to leave. There was Jack's boarding to see about first: it would have to be a place Abbie would approve of, with an outdoor run and the right sort of attendants. And there was the refrigerator to defrost, and the laundry to do, not to mention giving the place a thorough cleaning. And her car needed servicing. It hadn't run right since the storm, and it was already beginning to rust where it had been sandblasted.

One thing at a time. Reaching for the long strip of dust ruffle she'd already turned and pinned, she positioned it under the sewing-machine needle, adjusted the speed to fast forward, and pressed down on the foot pedal. Her eyes burned from overuse, saltwater, and a lack of sleep, and the bunnies were beginning to wriggle around in their gingham meadows again. If she never saw another damned rabbit, it would be too soon.

It happened so fast, she didn't realize it at first. There was no pain. Corey was still swearing at the jammed machine when she saw the broken sliver of steel that entered her forefinger just beside the nail.

A wave of sickness passed over her, and she swallowed hard and closed her eyes until it passed. "It doesn't hurt, it doesn't hurt," she muttered under her breath. "It's just a little sewing machine needle, all I have to do is yank it out."

Only it wouldn't yank. Bracing herself, Corey tugged on the broken end, but it was wedged in solidly. There was still no pain, but there was an increasing feeling of tightness that was growing more uncomfortable by the minute.

A doctor? Could she even drive that far? Goodness, she certainly didn't need a doctor for this. A mechanic, perhaps, but she'd treated far worse wounds on Winnie, and even on Ed. And what about all those animals she'd doctored under a veterinarian's instructions? The trouble was, the blasted thing was in her right hand, and she was no good with her left.

Like it or not, Rune was going to have to help her. One yank with a pair of pliers and it would be all over. It was a clean wound—a dab of disinfectant and she'd be as good as new. It was nothing compared with the fishhook she'd removed from Ed's backside the first year they were married.

She wasn't even decently dressed. Oh, blast, if she had to go and do something so stupid, why couldn't she have been wearing her salmon pink silk instead of her nightgown and Abbie's old faded-cotton housecoat? She couldn't change clothes with a needle sticking out of her finger. If it snagged, she'd die.

So much for that daydream she'd entertained about his remembering her as mysterious and glamorous. Gathering the tail of her pale blue nightgown up in her left hand, Corey shouldered her way out the door and headed for Rune's place. If he was out walking already, she'd just have to wait, because there wasn't a darned thing she could do in this condition.

"Rune? Are you there?" She called timidly through the screen door. When there was no answer after several tries, she let herself in and called through the kitchen door. The cottages were identical except for the furnishings.

"Rune? It's me, Corey. I need you."

Something struck the floor in the west bedroom, and she heard the sound of muffled cursing. So far, so good. At least he was home. "Rune, I'll just take a minute of your time, but it's something I can't handle alone."

Silently, he emerged from the bedroom, hair standing on end, a look so scaldingly cynical on his face that at first she didn't even notice that he was stark naked.

Corey swallowed twice in quick succession. Then, nailing her gaze somewhere just over his left shoulder, she blurted, "Could you—uh—would you mind putting something on?"

"Oh, we mustn't offend the lady's tender sensibilities, must we?" Rune sneered. "What's the matter, Mrs. Peters; haven't you ever seen a man in his natural state before?"

Once the initial shock had passed, Corey's anger began to escalate at a dizzying pace. Of all the crude, offensive, hateful—! Thank God she'd seen through him in time. To think she'd ever wasted a single minute's agony on this insufferable lout! "Look," she gritted evenly, her right hand clenched behind her, "I won't prolong this any more than you make it necessary. Believe me, if there were any alternative short of flagging down a passing motorist and taking my chances, I wouldn't be here now."

In spite of the hammers inside his skull, in spite of the disgust that curdled his guts, Rune had to admire her panache. Any other woman would have waited for a more romantic time of day. Not Corey. No champagne and roses this time, no siree! Instead of dolling up in something seductive and setting the scene, she barged in at the crack of dawn dressed in that rag Abbie wore to take out the trash and demanded a showdown. Probably thought she'd catch him off guard.

"Rune, *please?*" she gritted through clenched teeth.

"Sorry I can't produce any violin music. Would a dozen red roses, slightly used, help create the proper ambience?" With magnificent disregard for his unclothed state, he ambled across to the table and removed the battered roses from their container, a plastic milk carton. "A bit the worse for wear, I'm afraid," he apologized, bowing low as he presented them to her.

Corey snatched them with her left hand, ignoring his low groan, the grimace of pain, and the hand that pressed against his forehead as he straightened up.

"You stole my roses," she accused, placing them tenderly on the table. Granted, she'd crammed them into the trash can, another of her grand gestures, like pouring out his champagne, but even so . . . "You had no right to do that!"

"Lady, I don't know what the devil you're talking about, but would you please make your pitch and then get the hell out of here? If you were half as smart as I gave you credit for, you'd know that you've already cut your chances to one in a thousand with your rotten sense of timing."

The man was raving, ranting mad. A crook, a profligate, and if that empty bottle on the table was anything to go by, a drunk, as well. "All I want from you is a pair of pliers and a hand."

Rocking back on his heels, Rune stared owlishly. "God, I don't believe this," he whispered painfully. "You honestly expect me to—*pliers?* You have the unmitigated nerve to come here and—then what the hell were all those baby clothes for?"

"Look, could you please put a towel or something around you first?" She'd given up on trying to make sense from the babblings of a madman. If he didn't quit flaunting himself, she'd be babbling, too.

"Did you say *pliers?*" Rune repeated slowly.

"If you don't have any, I can probably locate a pair, but frankly, I didn't feel like jumbling around in Abbie's tool box in this condition." She held up her right hand, but Rune's horrified gaze was pinned to her stomach.

Her stomach? "Rune, please," she wailed. The man was not only a crude, unprincipled lout, and probably an alcoholic, he was a sadist! If she'd had anyone else to go to for help, she wouldn't have lowered her pride, and then, for him to torment her this way—!

Marching right up to within a foot of his magnificent naked body, Corey waved her forefinger under his nose. "You pull this damned thing out of my finger right this minute or I'll—I'll *hit* you with it!"

Assailed by several sensations at once, the warm, wildflower scent of her hair, the irresistible allure of her heaving bosom and her jutting lower lip, it took a moment for Rune's gaze to focus on the thing she was waving under his nose. When it did, he reacted with commendable swiftness.

He fainted.

Dismayed, Corey stared down at him. He'd gone down like an ox, so limp she was pretty sure he hadn't broken anything, but what did she do now? The man was crazy. He could wake up in a violent rage, and she'd be helpless against his superior strength.

Unbidden, her eyes strayed over the prone form at her feet, and she caught her bottom lip between her teeth. He looked so beautiful, lying there like a fallen gladiator. For a brief moment, she allowed herself the pleasure of studying the man who'd given her a glimpse of heaven and then snatched it away again.

"Why couldn't you have loved me, too?" she asked softly. "Why couldn't you have been real?" Sighing, she looked around for something to cover him with. For the first time, she noticed the packed suitcases, the lack of personal items in the room, and something inside her curled up into a tight, hard knot.

Holding the wrist of her right hand tightly with her left, Corey sat on the edge of the couch and sighed. If he didn't wake up in a couple of minutes, she'd probably have to do something. She was considering the merits of ice water versus cheek-slapping, not without a certain degree of pleasure, when Rune stirred and groaned.

Before she could direct her gaze away from his lean, virile body, his eyes opened. "There goes the macho image," he said with a trace of the gentle self-mockery she'd missed so much lately. If after all this, he suddenly reverted to the old Rune, the man she'd fallen head over heels in love with, she didn't think she could stand it.

"Are you all right?" she asked quietly.

Gingerly, he sat up, drawing one leg up and resting his arm across it while he studied her. The slow smile he sent her was almost like one of the old smiles, yet oddly tinged with sadness. "Yeah, sure. A few bruises on the old dignity, but other than that . . ." He shrugged. "Ironic, isn't it? You're the one in the delicate condition, and I'm the one who gets poleaxed."

"I'm sorry, Rune. I should have thought—I mean, some people can't take things like this, but I didn't know what else to do. You're the only one I could go to for help."

The smile shifted subtly, reflecting something less pleasant, and quite suddenly, Corey had had enough. She jumped up and dodged around the stack of luggage, intent on getting as far away as possible, needle or no needle. Dear Lord, she didn't have to take this!

"Corey! Come back here!" He was on his feet by the time she reached the door. "Corey, don't go! Wait!"

She was halfway home by the time he reached the screen, and she knew a moment's bitter triumph. Crazy he might be, but even Rune McLaughlin would draw the line at streaking across the driveway in the middle of the day, jaybird naked.

"What are you going to do?" he yelled across the intervening concrete.

"What I should have done in the first place," Corey yelled back. "Go out on the highway and flag down a motorist!"

"You're nuts! Do you hear me, woman, you're absolutely bonkers!"

"Oh, that's great!" Corey forced a laugh as she jammed her feet into her sandals. "That's really marvelous!"

"At least let me get the needle out of your finger first. Let me do that much for you."

On the steps, gown tail clutched in her left hand, forefinger of the right held up as though testing the wind, Corey paused. Get the needle out of my finger *first*? Crazy, crazy! Still, it might be my best bet. How many strangers would stop on the highway for a woman in a nightgown and a flapping housecoat, waving a pair of pliers?

He met her at the foot of his steps, and Corey glanced nervously around her. "Rune, don't you think you'd better get some clothes on first? I can wait another few minutes."

"Does it hurt much?"

"It just feels tight. I think the needle must have jammed right against the bone, so that—Rune? Are you all right?"

Inhaling deeply, Rune braced his shoulders and nodded. "No problem. Just don't say the words bone and needle so close together, will you? Wait here, I'll get a pair of pliers."

The operation took less than a minute. Sweat beaded Rune's forehead, and Corey watched him worriedly. Crazy or not, she loved the man. If he passed out again, she wasn't sure she could drag him up the stairs. "Now go get dressed, or you're going to have to take out a license and start charging admission."

"I don't think male strippers are legal in this county." His eyes, much too close to hers, glinted with amusement

174

before the shutters came down again. "Hadn't you better call a doctor? I could drive you to Morehead City."

"No need. I've had my tetanus booster, and it's a clean wound. A dab of iodine and I'll be fine."

"Well, don't you think you should at least lie down for a little while?"

He hadn't released her hand, and it occurred to Corey that if anyone could see her now, dressed in Abbie's castoffs, standing at the backdoor of an ocean cottage, holding hands with a shaggy-headed, naked savage, they'd swear she was the crazy one. "Rune, I'm all right. I—well, thanks." she ended helplessly.

Rune, damn it, if you don't let go of my hand I'm going to push you down on the concrete and climb all over you! "I see you're all packed to leave, so I won't keep you." Her eyes, always a little too clear, a little too revealing, looked everywhere but at the man who stood inches away, sunlight glinting on his broad shoulders, his wild, unruly hair, the bleached tips of his shaggy mustache.

"Corey, look, we've both acted like fools, but don't you think it's time we started behaving like responsibile adults? I've had time to think, and I want you to know that whatever happens, it's okay. No questions asked."

She waited, her heart suspended in her breast. There was a point to all he was intimating, but for the life of her, she didn't know what it was.

"Didn't you hear what I said?"

"I heard."

"Well? Is that all you've got to say?" He was still holding her hand, doing his best to look into her eyes, but she wasn't making it any easier for him. "Damn it, I told you I'm willing to marry you. If the baby's mine, that's great. If he's not, then that's okay, too, because he's

175

yours." He waited expectantly for her to melt into his arms with gratitude.

Slowly she lifted her face and stared directly into his eyes. It took a moment for her heart to resume beating. "Why you condescending, egotistical bastard. Is *that* what you think? Is *that* what this is all about? You know what you can do? You can take your proposal, your sanctimonious, patronizing proposal, and—and *stuff* it!"

Jerking her hand away, she stepped back, eyes blazing with anger, shimmering with quick moisture. As she whirled away, the faded flowered housecoat flying, the image that burned itself into her retina and into her heart was of a man who was either the world's biggest fool . . .

Or the world's dearest one.

11

Corey gambled on two things. First, that Rune would take time for a cold shower, a couple of aspirin, or possibly some black coffee before he came after her. *If* he came after her. She was going purely on instinct.

Second, she thought she could be dressed and out of there before he could accomplish all that. Because she wasn't going to make it easy on him. He'd hurt her too badly, and besides, there were still a lot of things to be worked out, things she'd better think through in advance.

For instance, she wasn't at all sure he'd care for the idea of instant grandfatherhood. From swinging bachelor to that particular milestone was no small step. She'd had trouble accepting it herself.

All the while thoughts were churning around in her mind, Corey was struggling into her clothes. Most of the things she'd bought so impulsively had proved wildly impractical for actual everyday wear. She grabbed the white jumpsuit and zipped herself into it while she was ramming her feet into her flat sandals. At least she was saved the five or ten minutes it used to take her to tame and put up her hair.

The little four-cylinder engine coughed twice and then settled down to a slightly asthmatic rhythm, and she backed out of the driveway and headed for Morehead City. First stop: the medical center. It wouldn't hurt to have Abbie's doctor take a look at her finger, although there was really nothing there to see.

That accomplished, she sat in the car and wondered what she was going to do with herself for the next few hours. There was some serious thinking to be done, and it was going to take all the self-control she could muster to keep herself safely on this side of the sound. But after her early morning exposure to Rune's . . . exposure, she knew it was her only chance to maintain any degree of objectivity.

She located a mechanic who was willing to look at, listen to, and advise her about her car, heard the dismal diagnosis, and tried not to reel at the estimate. "One day next week," she promised weakly, knowing it would have to be done, and the sooner the better.

She picked up a soft-shell crab sandwich and a container of milk and took them to a nearby marina, where she sat, gazing unseeingly at the swaying masts as she munched. Diligently, she tried to apply her mind to the problems at hand.

Did she really want to marry a man who considered her capable of such a thing? "Do you really want to go on breathing?" she asked herself sardonically.

Would desire and a sense of noblesse oblige on his part make up for the lack of love? Did it really matter? She'd take what she could get and be grateful for it, and if she paid the price in misery later on, it would be worth it.

It was dusk when she headed home. She'd exhausted the attractions of the small port city, exhausted herself, as well, but at least she'd gained a degree of perspective. She'd never have managed that with Rune so close by.

There was still the matter of Winnie, of course. Rune thought she was a child, and Corey was not looking forward to having to tell him that not only was she an adult, but a married, extremely pregnant adult. Which, fairly or not, could cast a certain shadow over Corey herself.

One look was enough to tell her that he was home. His car, that exotic-looking piece of machinery, had a faintly menacing air about it, and Corey switched off her headlights and coasted into her usual parking place. His windows were dark. He might be asleep. He'd been awfully hung over when she'd woken him up that morning.

Without taking time to analyze her decision, Corey headed for the beach. If they were going to have a showdown, she'd prefer it to be on neutral ground.

It wasn't long in coming. Seated just below the crest of the dune, she was aware of his presence even before he spoke.

"Have a nice day?" The banality held an undercurrent of malice that stirred goose bumps on her arms. So far, not so good.

"Oh, hi, Rune. How's your head?"

"I'll survive." He dropped down beside her, not

touching her, and Corey swallowed hard as she caught the subtle scent of his after-shave. "Has your finger bothered you?" he inquired politely.

"Not really. I had the doctor glance at it, but since my tetanus was up-to-date, there was really nothing that needed doing."

The silence slowly filled with small sounds: the shushing of the lazy surf, the cry of an occasional nocturnal sea bird. Corey wrapped her arms around her, feeling a chill that had nothing to do with the balmy evening breeze. Her stomach growled. "I had a marvelous soft-shell crab sandwich for lunch," she announced brightly.

"I could cheerfully throttle you, you know. Do you have any idea how many miles I drove, how many hours I spent searching for you? I'd have probably headed for Missouri except for that damned tomcat. I knew that not even you would go off and leave an animal to starve."

"Not even me?" She spoke the words slowly, wonderingly. Turning to face him, she repeated them. *"Not even me?"*

"Grammatically, I suppose it should be—"

"To hell with grammatically! I want to know what you mean by that nasty crack!"

The gloves were off, and it was no holds barred. "You want to know what I mean? I'll tell you what I mean! I mean, a woman who'd get herself pregnant and—"

"Get her*self* pregnant! Oh *ho!* Has ERA heard about this, I wonder?"

"Shut up, you—" He grabbed her by the shoulders, his fingers biting into the cool flesh. And then, groaning, he pulled her into his arms. "Oh, Corey, what are you doing to me? God, woman, I can't take much more of this."

His mustache was brushing against her ear, causing a wildly erotic response as her hormone level shot skyward. And then somehow, she was flat on her back, and he was leaning over her, his face in shadow so that she couldn't tell if he was still angry with her or not.

"Rune? There's something you'd better know before you go any further."

"You're out on parole, is that it? You pulled the London train job, and your name is on wanted lists in six countries. I don't care anymore." His lips followed the line of her jaw and then moved deftly to the corner of her mouth. "Corey, I just don't care—I want you more than I've ever wanted anything in my life, do you understand?"

"What about when I'm old and gray and surrounded by grandchildren?" With his hand on her zipper, grandchildren were the last thing on her mind.

"Haven't you ever heard—" The zipper undone, his hands began a journey of exploration. "—that old saw about snow on the roof?"

Corey felt her breasts swell and harden under his touch, and she curled her fingers frantically into the pelt on his chest.

"There's a blazing inferno in my furnace, darling, enough to keep us both warm for a lot of years to come," he promised gruffly. His mouth took hers, forestalling any remark she might have made.

Words could never have expressed what Corey was feeling. A language older than the spoken word blazed between them, in the trembling touch of his hand on her breast, the wondering caress of her hand on his face. Lifting himself away from her, Rune ripped off his shirt and spread it carefully over the sand. And then he lifted

her, centering her body on the fabric that still held th
warmth of his. His eyes never leaving her, he remove
his jeans, and Corey caught her breath at the shee
beauty of his bare flanks in the dim light of a phosphores
cent surf.

"One of these days you're going to find yourself—
what was it? The star attraction on the court docket?" sh
teased, lifting her feet for him to finish removing he
pants.

"As long as you're the female lead, it'll be worth it. Ak
Corey, you're so lovely . . . you're made of moonligh
all midnight dark and silvery pale. Let me love you
darling."

Even knowing that the word was meant only in
limited sense, she hugged it to her heart. Oh, yes, lov
me, my dearest Rune, and let me love you in all the way
I know how.

The touch of his hands on her body was incendiary
the touch of his lips, his tongue; sheer, glorious madness
Corey writhed as he poured kisses down the sensitiv
slopes of her breasts, tasted and stroked and suckled the
rigid, throbbing points. Following the imperceptible tra
that led down the center of her torso, he burnished he
with soft-edged kisses that sent flames shooting to th
very center of her being.

His tongue reamed her navel, and she moaned. Sh
wanted to touch him, to taste him, to arouse him as h
was arousing her, but he left her weak and trembling
drifting on a sea of the purest sensation as the magic c
his kisses moved nearer and nearer their hidden goal.

"Ah, Rune, you mustn't . . ." she sighed.

"Be still, my dearest heart, and let me make you
bloom."

182

And he did. And as she felt herself carried higher and higher on a tidal wave of incredible pleasure, he moved swiftly to join her, and together, they rode higher still, meeting drive with thrust, until finally, clinging, tumbling, holding fast, they laughed and sobbed together for the sheer joy of living.

Long afterward, she lay in his arms, heedless of the sand that stuck to her damp skin, uncaring of everything but the quiet thunder of his heart beating under her cheek, his lips in her hair. "I wish there was something I could do about loving you so much, Rune, but I can't. I'm sorry—I'll try not to be a nuisance with it."

There was a sudden stillness, and then, like the sound of tearing cloth, the air ripped into his lungs. "Would you mind repeating what you just said? I think I must have sand in my ears." His voice was thick with disbelief and something that defied interpretation.

"I know how men are about these things. And we're older, so it's not as though—"

"How *are* men? About *what* things? Let's be specific, shall we?"

"You know. About romance, and love and—well, *talking* about it." She squirmed uncomfortably. A unilateral discussion of the tenderer emotions wasn't exactly her cup of tea, either, come to think of it.

"Now, wait a minute, isn't that a leading assumption? I'd say you've completely overlooked every piece of evidence at your disposal."

"Oh, don't go all legal on me. I simply meant that yes, I'll marry you if you still want me, and no, I won't expect any hearts and flowers . . ." She grinned into the darkness. "Especially if you're going to steal them back. And," she rushed on before her courage deserted her,

"I'm not pregnant. All those baby things are for my grandchild. In less than five months, I'm going to be a grandmother."

Closing her eyes, she clenched her teeth and waited. If he called off the whole game and took his clothes and went home, she'd understand. It would probably kill her, but she'd understand. After all, he didn't have to marry her now. No one was holding a shotgun on him any longer.

In the stillness, a mosquito droned ominously. The annoying sound ceased just as Rune began to laugh. His whole body shook with the force of it. He howled, sitting up, and then falling back on the sandy shirt. Corey waited. The mosquito found a vulnerable area on her hip and began drilling, and it was a moment before she even felt it.

"Rune?" she ventured finally, brushing the blood thirsty insect away. "Does this mean you're not . . . too upset?"

Bracing himself on one elbow, he hung over her, the gleam of a grin splitting the dark shadow of his face. "Corey. My wonderful, wicked, darling Corey. No, I'm not upset. Remind me to dig out my model train set for our grandson when we go back to Raleigh, though, will you?"

"I'd sort of counted on a granddaughter."

"Looks like our Winnie's going to be pretty busy for the next few years, doesn't it?" Rune nuzzled her throat and then yelped. "Look, could we move this family planning session inside?" he demanded, slapping his backside and then scratching. "Those little dive-bombers are getting too personal for comfort."

"Does this mean you still want to marry me?" Corey

184

asked as soon as they reached the safety of the screened porch.

Dropping their sandy clothes in a heap on the floor, Rune gathered her into his arms. "What have I been telling you? What does it take to convince you? I'm a pretty eloquent guy, given the proper incentive, but sweetheart, the only words I know are the plain old-fashioned ones. I love you more than I ever knew it was possible to love another human being."

Corey caught her breath, hardly daring to believe him lest she suddenly wake up and find that it was all a dream of her own desperate making.

"Want more, huh? Then, how about this? Your children are my children, your grandchildren mine. Of course, that works both ways. My mother is now yours. Think you can handle Helen as a mother-in-law?"

"I'll tell you after I've met her," said Corey, far too happy to let a little thing like a dreadnought of a mother-in-law worry her now.

"But haven't you—I mean, aren't you . . . ?" He let the question hang there until Corey, a little slow on the uptake, picked it up.

"You mean you still think that I was sent here by your mother to trick you into matrimony? My goodness, Rune, if you actually believe that . . ." She laughed delightedly. "No wonder you were so reluctant. Is that what this has all been about? Your fits of temperament, your on-again, off-again friendship? I thought I was going crazy, did you know that? And then I thought *you* were."

"Precious, at this point, I don't care if you were sent by a whole Senate subcommittee. If you love me, that's all that matters."

A flash of headlights sent them scurrying for cover.

Laughing, Corey said, "If we're going to be spending much time at the beach in the foreseeable future, I'd recommend a longer driveway."

"Yeah," Rune grunted. "Or a moat with a draw-bridge." He was reaching through the backdoor with the broom in an attempt to snag his jeans and drag them into the kitchen. "Were you expecting company?"

Corey was hurriedly twisting the buttons of Abbie's housecoat into whatever buttonholes were handiest. "No, were you? Look, hide in here, and I'll get rid of them, whoever it is."

The rattling pounding on the screen door was accompanied by a vaguely familiar voice calling her name. "Miz Peters? You home?"

Hurriedly, Corey presented herself, thankful that she hadn't yet turned on the lights. "Who is it? Oh. Don't I know you?"

"Keever's Delivery Service, ma'am. I don't normally run this late, but I start summer school next week, and—"

"You delivered my roses," Corey declared. "And come to think of it, weren't you the one who delivered the champagne, too?"

"That wuz me, all right, ma'am. See, the thing is, I promised Miss Abbie I'd deliver these things on a full moon, but the trouble is, I can't wait for this next one. This here's a five-pound box of candy, one for you, and one for the gent next door, like always. Could I leave 'em both here? If I left his on the porch, it'd be chocolate syrup by the time the sun was up good, and if he's a late sleeper, the ants would get to it before he did."

Somehow Corey managed to contain herself until the delivery boy had backed out of the driveway. She could feel Rune's presence just inside the kitchen. Clutching the two boxes of chocolates, she stood it as long as she could, and then she collapsed into one of the sagging wicker chairs, laughing until tears streamed down her cheeks.

"Did you hear?"

"Would you please contain yourself long enough to hand me my pants?"

"He's gone, you can come out now, but Rune, did you *hear* that? Do you know what it *means?*"

"It means," Rune declared firmly, marching mother-naked out onto the porch to claim his property, "that you didn't send me that cheap champagne, after all, and that you didn't send me those red roses, and that we've both been set up by a pair of the slickest operators this side of—"

"The Mississippi," Corey choked. "Oh, Rune, it's priceless! No wonder Abbie was so insistent. No wonder she kept asking me if I'd started dating again."

"And my mother, letting me think she was heartbroken because I'd run off without telling her where I was. Me. Thirty-nine-years-old, and I still can't outwit that woman. I'm embarrassed, if you want to know the truth. A thing like that . . . well, it could unman a guy."

Corey rose to the occasion willingly. Gathering him in her arms, she held him tightly, burying her face in the wiry, sandy hair on his chest. "Darling, your mother just wants you to be happy. Don't begrudge her that privilege. And as for the other, the unmanning, I think I can set your mind at ease on that score."

His body stirred against her, and suddenly, she was the one who was being held. "Now that, my friend and lover, is the best offer I've had all night. If you'd care to disrobe and step this way, I think a long, leisurely bath is in order."

"What about the sand in the plumbing?" Corey asked, her fingers busy undoing the buttons she'd just done up.

"Under the circumstances, I don't think Abbie would mind too much, do you?"

As the light from a newly risen moon—far from full—crept over their entwined bodies much later, Corey wondered if Winnie would consider the names of Helen and Abigail too old-fashioned for a baby girl.

WIN

a fabulous $50,000 diamond jewelry collection

ENTER

by filling out the coupon below and mailing it by September 30, 1985

Send entries to:

U.S.
Silhouette Diamond Sweepstakes
P.O. Box 779
Madison Square Station
New York, NY 10159

Canada
Silhouette Diamond Sweepstakes
Suite 191
238 Davenport Road
Toronto, Ontario M5R 1J6

SILHOUETTE DIAMOND SWEEPSTAKES
ENTRY FORM

☐ Mrs.   ☐ Miss   ☐ Ms   ☐ Mr.

NAME   (please print)

ADDRESS   APT. #

CITY

STATE/(PROV.)

ZIP/(POSTAL CODE)

RTD-A-1

RULES FOR SILHOUETTE DIAMOND SWEEPSTAKES

OFFICIAL RULES—NO PURCHASE NECESSARY

1. Silhouette Diamond Sweepstakes is open to Canadian (except Quebec) and United States residents 18 years or older at the time of entry. Employees and immediate families of the publishers of Silhouette, their affiliates, retailers, distributors, printers, agencies and RONALD SMILEY INC. are excluded.

2. To enter, print your name and address on the official entry form or on a 3" x 5" slip of paper. You may enter as often as you choose, but each envelope must contain only one entry. Mail entries first class in Canada to Silhouette Diamond Sweepstakes, Suite 191, 238 Davenport Road, Toronto, Ontario M5R 1J6. In the United States, mail to Silhouette Diamond Sweepstakes, P.O. Box 779, Madison Square Station, New York, NY 10159. Entries must be postmarked between February 1 and September 30, 1985. Silhouette is not responsible for lost, late or misdirected mail.

3. First Prize of diamond jewelry, consisting of a necklace, ring, bracelet and earrings will be awarded. Approximate retail value is $50,000 U.S./$62,500 Canadian. Second Prize of 100 Silhouette Home Reader Service Subscriptions will be awarded. Approximate retail value of each is $162.00 U.S./$180.00 Canadian. No substitution, duplication, cash redemption or transfer of prizes will be permitted. Odds of winning depend upon the number of valid entries received. One prize to a family or household. Income taxes, other taxes and insurance on First Prize are the sole responsibility of the winners.

4. Winners will be selected under the supervision of RONALD SMILEY INC., an independent judging organization whose decisions are final, by random drawings from valid entries postmarked by September 30, 1985, and received no later than October 7, 1985. Entry in this sweepstakes indicates your awareness of the Official Rules. Winners who are residents of Canada must answer correctly a time-related arithmetical skill-testing question to qualify. First Prize winner will be notified by certified mail and must submit an Affidavit of Compliance within 10 days of notification. Returned Affidavits or prizes that are refused or undeliverable will result in alternative names being randomly drawn. Winners may be asked for use of their name and photo at no additional compensation.

5. For a First Prize winner list, send a stamped self-addressed envelope postmarked by September 30, 1985. In Canada, mail to Silhouette Diamond Contest Winner, Suite 309, 238 Davenport Road, Toronto, Ontario M5R 1J6. In the United States, mail to Silhouette Diamond Contest Winner, P.O. Box 182, Bowling Green Station, New York, NY 10274. This offer will appear in Silhouette publications and at participating retailers. Offer void in Quebec and subject to all Federal, Provincial, State and Municipal laws and regulations and wherever prohibited or restricted by law.

READERS' COMMENTS ON SILHOUETTE DESIRES

"Thank you for Silhouette Desires. They are the best thing that has happened to the bookshelves in a long time."

—V.W.*, Knoxville, TN

"Silhouette Desires—wonderful, fantastic—the best romance around."

—H.T.*, Margate, N.J.

"As a writer as well as a reader of romantic fiction, I found DESIREs most refreshingly realistic—and definitely as magical as the love captured on their pages."

—C.M.*, Silver Lake, N.Y.

"I just wanted to let you know how very much I enjoy your Silhouette Desire books. I read other romances, and I must say your books rate up at the top of the list."

—C.N.*, Anaheim, CA

"Desires are number one. I especially enjoy the endings because they just don't leave you with a kiss or embrace; they finish the story. Thank you for giving me such reading pleasure."

—M.S.*, Sandford, FL

*names available on request